LYNNE TRUSS is one of Britain's best-loved comic writers and is the author of the worldwide bestsellers *Eats, Shoots & Leaves* and *Talk to the Hand*. Her most recent book is *Get Her Off the Pitch!* She reviews for the *Sunday Times* and writes regularly for radio.

From the reviews of *A Certain Age*:

'Sensationally well written – funny, poignant and beautifully observed'
The Times

'Dazzling . . . sad, funny and, of course, exquisitely written'
Daily Mail

'Beautifully observed . . . Truss is simply a huge talent'
Guardian

'Good grief, she's funny . . . A total delight'
KATE SAUNDERS, *The Times*

'Top-quality writing'
Sunday Times

'She has an impeccable ear for dialogue and the entangled poignancy and farce of the human condition' *Glasgow Herald*

D1371937

By the same author:

With One Lousy Free Packet of Seed

*Making the Cat Laugh: One Woman's Journal of
Single Life on the Margins*

Tennyson's Gift

Going Loco

Tennyson and His Circle

*Eats, Shoots & Leaves: The Zero Tolerance Approach
to Punctuation*

*Talk to the Hand: The Utter Bloody Rudeness of Everyday Life
(or Six Good Reasons to Stay Home and Bolt the Door)*

*A Certain Age: Twelve Monologues from the Classic
Radio Series*

Get Her Off the Pitch!: How Sport Took Over My Life

FOR CHILDREN

*Eats, Shoots & Leaves: Why, Commas Really Do Make
a Difference!*

*The Girl's Like Spaghetti: Why, You Can't Manage
Without Apostrophes!*

Twenty-Odd Ducks: Why, Every Punctuation Mark Counts!

LYNNE TRUSS

A Certain Age

FOURTH ESTATE · *London*

Fourth Estate
An imprint of HarperCollins*Publishers*
77–85 Fulham Palace Road
Hammersmith
London W6 8JB

Visit our authors' blog at www.fifthestate.co.uk
Love this book? www.bookarmy.com

This Fourth Estate paperback edition published 2010
1

First published in Great Britain by Profile Books in 2007.

Copyright © Miraculous Panda, 2007

Lynne Truss asserts the moral right to be identified as the author of this work

A catalogue record for this book is available from the British Library

ISBN 978-0-00-735524-2

Designed by Geoff Green Book Design, Cambridge
Typeset in Swift by MacGuru Ltd

Printed and bound in Great Britain by Clays Ltd, St Ives plc

Mixed Sources
Product group from well-managed
forests and other controlled sources
www.fsc.org Cert no. SW-COC-001806
© 1996 Forest Stewardship Council

FSC is a non-profit international organisation established to promote the
responsible management of the world's forests. Products carrying the FSC
label are independently certified to assure consumers that they come
from forests that are managed to meet the social, economic and
ecological needs of present and future generations.

Find out more about HarperCollins and the environment at
www.harpercollins.co.uk/green

All rights reserved. No part of this publication may be reproduced,
stored in a retrieval system, or transmitted, in any form or by any means,
electronic, mechanical, photocopying, recording or otherwise,
without the prior permission of the publishers.

This book is sold subject to the condition that it shall not, by way of trade
or otherwise, be lent, re-sold, hired out or otherwise circulated without the
publisher's prior consent in any form of binding or cover other than that
in which it is published and without a similar condition including
this condition being imposed on the subsequent purchaser.

Contents

Introduction

These monologues were written for BBC Radio Four, and appeared in two series. The first, which comprised all the female voices, was broadcast in 2002. The second series (the men) followed in 2005. Many were written specifically for the actors who played them, so to that extent are collaborations. All were produced by Dawn Ellis, of BBC Radio's Light Entertainment department, who put as much of her heart and soul into them as I did. Since the whole point of a monologue is that it should speak for itself, I hope these pieces don't require much by way of introduction. I'd just like to mention a few things to put them in context.

Since the advent of the video diary, we've become so accustomed to stories told in this particular straight-to-audience form that you could be forgiven for assuming (as I did when I started writing mine) that it had been knocking around since ancient times. How those Athenian theatre festival-goers were delighted, for example, when, over a series of well-crafted scenes, the goddess Athena endured and reported (to no one in particular) the roller-coaster emotions involved in setting up her successful high-street poster company. But, in fact, no such play seems to have come down to us. When Alan Bennett wrote his first *Talking Heads* in the late 1980s, it seems he was pioneering a quite new dramatic form.

Up to that point, a "monologue" could mean any number of things: to a student actor, it was any uninter-rupted speech learned for audition purposes; to a literary critic, it was a type of Victorian poem. Of course, there were stage monologues, both in the legitimate theatre and in the music hall, but they were unlike Bennett's in two respects: first, they were generally addressed to a particular, unseen person; and second, they were fixed in time. As recently as 1983, a critic wrote that the monologue "lacks the resources to develop the temporal dimension, the notion of life as a continuing process of growth and change". But then Bennett came along and divided his monologues into scenes, and suddenly the temporal dimension was added, just like that. There was a simple fade to black, then a fade up again. At a stroke, this completely changed the kind of story that could be told.

My own monologue career started in the mid-1990s, when I was asked to write scripts for the Natural History Unit in Bristol. A radio series called *Dear Sir ... Yours, Ruffled* was to put the case for six unloved common British species, by having them voice their own story, as if in rather furious letters to *The Times*. My job was to tackle two of these stout defences: an urban fox, for Tony Robinson, and a grey squirrel, for June Whitfield. Instantly, I was in heaven. "Do you think that old teabag is going begging?"

the fox interrupted himself, before he gulped it down. I had him shudder at the thought of Basil Brush: "Those dead eyes, you know, like buttons." And in between the jokes, of course, there was lots of natural history information, such as the disgusting news that people used to rub squirrel brain on the gums of teething babies.

A series called *Tidal Talk from a Rock Pool* followed (I had nothing to do with these titles), and I had another field day with that. We had Bill Wallis playing a periwinkle, Geoffrey Palmer as a hermit crab, Alison Steadman as an anemone ("My enemy's anemone is my friend"), Greg Proops as a goby fish, Judi Dench as a limpet and Tony Robinson as a lugworm. I made the periwinkle a kind of music hall comedian trying to cheer up all the others. "So the big shark says, 'Here's that sick squid I owe you', ha ha. All right, suit yourselves; I'm wasted here."

The animal I cared most about in that series was the limpet: stuck, lonely and bitter, on its rock while the salt waves surged and the far horizon beckoned. "Moscow! Moscow! Moscow!" she cried. She browsed algae from the rock, gossiped about the lewdness of the American slipper limpet, and quoted from Tennyson and Oscar Wilde. Judi Dench chose a Celia Johnson voice, which was superb; she also gamely stuffed her cheeks with Maltesers to represent the algae-browsing activity. The limpet went for a short walk, which meant she had to lift her shell and shuffle an inch or two, making comical straining and exertion noises. "I don't know if you've ever had the misfortune to befriend a limpet," she confided in a whisper, "but they are notoriously hard to shake off." She remembered in despair that her mother once upbraided her, in her youth, for her unfortunate habit of "dwelling on things".

Maybe I've been making heavy weather of this monologue-writing, but the image of the limpet blindly shuffling its shell along, while panting and groaning, does quite resemble what it was like to inhabit each of the twelve characters in this book. You may have seen the movie *Being John Malkovich*, in which a mysterious portal behind a filing cupboard allows people to occupy the brain of John Malkovich for ten minutes at a time, seeing the world through his eyes, and then (if they concentrate very, very hard), getting him to say things, or move his arm. Writing monologues is similar to that. I've varied the form as much as I can in these twelve: there are plotty ones and organic ones; twisty and straightforward; light and dark; redemptive and non-redemptive. One of them – "The Husband" – is simply exposition. But all of them required the same strenuous mental puppeteering. These are not all nice people, by the way; but that's part of the point of doing it.

From the technical point of view, what I was most surprised to learn about the monologue is that there are all sorts of stories that can't be told this way. In proposing the men's series, for example, I came up with this idea for "The Son", which turned out to be unworkable:

The Son

Jason is a Kiwi vet, unmarried, straight, and popular with the pet-ladies of his West Country parish because of his understanding tone. They are all in love with him: he seems to be refreshingly in touch with his "feminine side". It doesn't even bother them when their pets fail to flourish under his care. But when he learns that his mother has died in New Zealand, he goes to pieces, and is dropped by everyone. It turns out that his feminine-side appeal has limits.

Tone: arch
Theme: access to "feminine" emotions
Ideal casting: Martin Clunes

Now, there are problems with this that anyone can spot – Martin Clunes with a New Zealand accent being just one of them. But the main problem is that the protagonist of this story can't actually tell it, because it's mainly about how he is unconsciously perceived by other people. If he *knows* these women all adore him for his feminine side, the theme stops being "access to emotions" and becomes manipulativeness or even vanity. Anyway, I quickly dropped this idea, and instead wrote a "Son" that was about a light-hearted photographer's very happy and matter-of-fact relationship with his dead father, which was possibly my favourite of the whole twelve.

By way of counter-example, there is this:

The Married Man

Jim is an American mystery writer living in London. His stories are middlebrow puzzle mysteries, and he enjoys being the omniscient author in command of all the facts. In his personal life, he is conducting a casual long-term affair which he thinks his wife doesn't know about. She does. She also always guesses "whodunnit" by about the 50th page, which ought to tell him something about how smart she is. In the end, of course, it's his own inability to pick up clues that is his downfall.

Tone: light
Theme: control
Ideal casting: Kevin Spacey

This proposal bears a pretty close resemblance to the piece as it turned out, except for the madly unrealistic Kevin Spacey thing. The reason it worked was that its theme was, actually, not control but self-deception. The characters in this book all speak for themselves, but the interest for the person reading or listening to them is always, primarily, in ascertaining and judging how well they know or understand their own story. Alan Bennett describes his *Talking Heads* characters as people who "don't quite know what they are saying, and are telling a story to the meaning of which they are not entirely privy". After I'd completed the second series of *A Certain Age*, I went to see the excellent revival of Christopher Hampton's *The Philanthropist*, in which a character says there are only two types of people in the world: those who live by what they know to be a lie; and those who live by what they believe, falsely, to be the truth. This stark assessment of humanity applies perfectly to the protagonists of dramatic monologues. "We don't live our lives for other people," Judy is happy to parrot in "The Daughter". And she believes it, even though living for someone else is precisely what she's doing.

I ought to explain why it's called *A Certain Age*. The idea for the original series arose out of my rather weak observation that in one's early forties, a person comes to realise that some particular life choices are no longer open. In fact, many life choices seem already to have been made, sometimes without the involvement of any conscious decision. Thus, a woman might find she could define herself at age forty-two as the mother of a grown-up daughter, or the daughter of an elderly parent, or a wife of twenty-five years. Always keen to impose technical limits on myself, I decided that this system – Mother, Daughter, Wife, etc. – would discipline me, in that each person would talk about just one central relationship. At that time, incidentally, I thought the phrase "a certain age" would have a nice double meaning, in that your forties also bring you more confidence in knowing who you are. However, except in the case of the contented Cat Lover, and the happily restored Pedant, the narrators are subject to the usual curse of the monologue, in that (see above) they don't know quite what they're saying, and don't know the full story anyway.

I wish there were a better, more attractive term than "monologue". What a turn-off word it is. It has any number of associations, and not one of them is pleasant. "And now Miss Truss has agreed to delight us with one of her monologues!" is the cue for any sane person to tip-toe to the hall, grab a coat at random, and then dash out into the stormy night. But at least banging on about monologues here makes one thing clear. The following are not first-person-narrated short stories. Despite the extraordinary talent the characters sometimes have for remembered dialogue, despite all their unlikely mastery of exposition, these are still slices of drama as opposed to slices of fiction. The way to differentiate the two forms is, by the way, quite simple.

"It was the tragedy of my father's death that it brought my family together."

That is the first line of a first-person-narrated short story.

"It was the tragedy of my father's death that it brought my family together, or I'm not riding this bike."

That is the first line of a monologue.

Finally, a word about the performances. If by any chance you pick up *A Certain Age* on BBC Audio, you will discover what an outstanding job was done in studio by each of our twelve great actors (listed on page 187). Casting *A Certain Age* was a nail-biting exercise, as it always is for radio, since actors' agents won't allow their stars to commit to radio work more than about three weeks ahead, in case something more lucrative comes up. But if the waiting is stressful, the reward is all the greater when your perfect actor actually steps into the studio with his *Guardian* under his arm and a copy of the script with bits already underlined. I am the soppiest of the soppy when it comes to actors, so I'd better not describe all the ecstatic dancing-on-the-spot I've been known to do when the actor has gone. But since I wrote these pieces for performance, I can hardly claim not to care about how absolutely brilliantly they were done.

A Note on the Text

When editing these pieces to make them identical with the edited broadcast versions, I found that I couldn't bear to lose (again) some of the precious incidental stuff I had bravely sacrificed in the cause of the rigid 28-minute time-slot. The text does, therefore, sometimes depart from the audio versions – but never for very long.

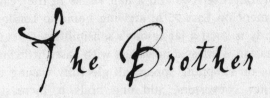

The Brother

TIM is quite posh; he is in the art business, a bit camp, and a natural loner. It will be for the listener to decide whether he is gay. Having inherited his father's gallery on the death of his parents, he has built up the dealership and takes great pride in his achievement. His older brother Julian lives in Australia. They have not met for ten years.

Scene One: at home; classical music playing quietly. Tim is jetlagged but very pleased with himself

No matter how many times you experience this, it's still horribly disorientating. Here I am, 9.30 in the evening, at home in Belsize Park, eighteenth-century mahogany desk piled high with post opened in my absence by the lovely Gideon, and this morning – well, this morning I was crossing Fifth Avenue in a yellow cab, on the way to

Newark (because, of course, I never use JFK). [*Yawn*] It's too brutal! After two and a half weeks in the Peabody apartment on East 75th, arriving home to London so abruptly is SUCH a jar to one's sensibilities. Of course, Manhattan is infested nowadays with nasty little British people on shopping sprees, all gleefully waving their currency converters, and one finds it increasingly difficult to avoid them, alas, even in the smarter galleries on Madison. The woman in the adjacent seat on the flight home – and this was in UPPER, as they so unpleasantly denominate it these days – told me she had bought [*he remembers the details precisely, but they don't mean much to him*] ten mini iPods in assorted colours and a suitcase full of Region 1 DVDs. I said, [*very condescending*] "How lovely. And did that take you long?" And she told me she had been in Manhattan only TWO DAYS; she'd just "popped over" while her husband was on the Algarve playing golf. I said, "Oh I bought very little for myself, I'm afraid. But then I do travel to New York several times a year." And she said, [*scoff; not an imitation*] "So do I, dear! This day flight's much better than the night one, innit? That night one does my head in."

[*He riffles through post*] So. What have we here? [*Shuffles and yawns as he talks*] American Express, something tedious from Balliol; begging letter, begging letter [*tears up the begging letters*]; *Art Quarterly*; oh, cheque; ooh, NICE cheque; [*less happy*] mmm, small cheque, I sold that Ravanelli drawing much too cheaply; National Gallery invitation; cheque, ooh, VERY nice cheque; letter from [*surprised, when he checks the signature*] Julian, that's odd, I'd better read that; small cheque, gallery invitation, gallery invitation; one, two, THREE copies of the *Spectator* (hurrah), and – ugh, well, a lot more that I'll concern myself with tomorrow, with the help of the lovely Gideon. [*Yawn*] I can't wait to show Gideon the Maffei sketch I bought from Fowlers and Wells. He's got quite an EYE, I think. [*Yawn*] Oh well, what does Julian want? [*He picks up Julian's letter, which is three pages, and scans bits of it*] It's unlike him not to e-mail. Post from Australia takes such an age. The funny thing is, with Julian's annual e-mails, I can always picture him in some internet café on Bondi, with palm umbrellas and towering surf, and a big cocktail standing by – probably one with an obscene name. I can just hear him ordering it: [*impersonates Julian, who is very commanding as well as louche*] "I want a Criminally Long Sweaty Screw, please, barman."

[*Yawn*] I really must go to bed soon. Oh well. [*Rustle*] "Dear Timmy." Well, [*puts letter down*] he does that to annoy me, of course, and also to be Big Brotherish. No one else even calls me Tim any more; I insist on T.J. – or even, with certain friends, "Teedge". Typical of the parents to cook up such a perfect imperious name for Julian and then just lose interest when I come along. Imagine being called Tim. Ugh. Imagine it, in particular, during Wimbledon fortnight! "Come on, Tim!" they all shout. "Come on, Tim!" Every year, in the weeks preceding the championships, the newspapers ask, "Is this the year for ... TIM?" And I say, "Look! No tournament besides tiddly-winks will ever be won by a person named Tim!" [*Pause*] They call him TimBO sometimes, you know. Now, that's enough to make you WEEP.

[*He has finished the rant; yawn*] So. "Dear Timmy," writes Julian. [*Very big yawn*] "I called last week and spoke to some bloke called Gideon." Bloke? Gideon is hardly a bloke, Julian, honestly. [*Peruses other pages*] I have to say, though, this is suspiciously well spelled and punctuated for Julian. The miracle of spellcheck, no doubt. [*Resumes reading*] "He told me you were in New York but would be home on 17th. I am writing because I have been thinking about a few things." [*Mutter*] Not before time, I'd say. "I realise I have never been a proper older brother to you." [*Tim is a bit disturbed by where this is going*] What's he talking about? A proper older brother? Julian was always a proper older brother to me. When we were at school he used to trip me going into assembly, steal my hymn book every Sunday, and punch me in the kidneys after nets; that's almost a definition of being a proper older brother. "I wonder if I ought to come back to London. I wonder if I should be [*Tim tightens with alarm, which increases as he continues*] helping you with father's art business. After all, I am technically head of the family."

Good heavens. [*Attempt at light-hearted laugh*] He makes us sound like the Corleones. Head of the family! "I'm sorry to say that Janey and I have parted." Oh no. Oh Julian, you idiot. Janey was so RICH. "She is using Arabella and Max as leverage, which has been quite unpleasant, not to say ruinously expensive. So I just thought, remember how father used to admire my EYE, Timmy?" No, I don't, as it happens. He admired MY eye, Julian. It was your FINGERS that made the biggest impression on father. When they were found in someone else's till. "Why don't I help you out for a few months in London? I never complained when you took over the gallery without me, did I?" What? You were in PRISON, Julian. [*Turns page*] "I've shown father's will to a few people and everyone thinks I've been quite negligent of my own interests. I mean, little Timmy's gambles have paid off well so far, so well done! But I'm a divorced man now, with titanic alimony. And you do [*ominous for Tim*] OWE ME, don't you?" Oh God. Oh no. [*Turns page*] "Arriving on 20th. Looking forward to working with you. Don't worry! My embezzling days are behind me. Besides, if I had any designs on your readies, little brother, I wouldn't need to travel halfway round the world, would I? I could clean you out without leaving my desk! Your loving older brother, Julian. PS If you managed to acquire any coloured iPods or Region 1 DVDs on your trip to New York, there are people in China who would be in the market."

[*A comical moan of fear and anxiety*] Uuugh.

Scene Two: out of doors, birds singing; traffic. Tim is sitting in a London square

[*Feverish*] I have two days. Two days to decide whether to hire a hitman. Of all the options presenting themselves, swift, clean assassination is clearly the most satisfactory. I spent most of last night running through the possibilities, and that was the conclusion that finally, at 5 a.m., allowed me to go to sleep. I mean, here are the options:

One. Sell business, feign own death in elaborate boating accident; start again in Panama.

Two. Lure Julian into gallery basement and dispatch him with own two hands.

Three. Persuade the lovely Gideon to lure Julian into basement, to dispatch with HIS own two hands.

Four. Give Julian indecently large sum to go away.

Five. Contrive to foil Julian by doing something a bit more subtle that at present eludes me.

Six. Undergo emergency plastic surgery and adopt Danish accent.

Seven. Engage moral pariah in motorcycle helmet with gun.

Of course it does occur to me that I'm over-reacting. This is where a partner would be invaluable. A partner would say, "He's your brother, T.J. You share a full genetic identity. What's yours is already his in a way. And he can't be as bad as all that. He's just got a small history of appropriating other people's money; plus, being your older brother he naturally has no respect for you; and of course he drew the long straw at the font. But don't forget, you haven't actually seen him for ten years, and people change." [*Pause*] I'm quite glad I DON'T have a partner, actually, if that's the sort of thundering drivel they would come up with. All I can think of, over and over, is the expression, "head of the family"! Head of the family? When there are only two of us? [*He's losing it*] Julian is just so clever at knowing how to – well, how to seriously upset me! For example, that was a split infinitive, wasn't it? "To seriously upset me" is a split infinitive. And I never split an infinitive unless I am very, very upset!

[*Deep breath; slower*] I'm seeing the solicitor at two. Douglas Devereaux at Collins, Bracknell in Queen Street; we were at Balliol together, I was his understudy on the cup-winning ping-pong team; he buys the odd French pastel from me for his highly acquisitive wife Marian and somehow always gets a discount whereas oddly I've NEVER had a discount from him. I called him first thing, of course, and he confirmed instantly what I already suspected: that Julian has no legal claim on the gallery, or on me. He said I was probably worrying about nothing. I said, [*trying to be light about it*] well, if I am, I'm doing it extremely efficiently, Dougie [*pronounced "Doogie"*]: I've already put all my personal bank accounts into the company name and shredded the evidence of the transfer, and sent Gideon to courier the more valuable items to Paris on the 11.58 Eurostar. It's no wonder I didn't get much sleep last night. Dougie said, [*Edinburgh accent*] "T.J., it's as if you're expecting a hurricane; have you taped up the windows as well?" [*Pause*] Well, he knows I loathe sarcasm. "Oh, come in at two," he said.

He's a good chap, Dougie, with an innocent passion for patisserie, and he's got a beautiful King Charles spaniel who sleeps at his feet like something from a crusader's tomb. One does quietly object, however, to paying a thousand pounds a minute for Dougie's time when he allows himself personal asides and little flights of fancy on one's bill, as it were. [*Dougie*] "I'd like to say embezzlement is an ugly word, T.J.," he said. "But when you think about it – well, it's quite a nice one, isn't it? Quite musical. Em-bezzle-ment. Mm, interesting." You see, if a friend were to say that, one could shrug and think, "What a peculiar mind that chap must have." But when one's solicitor says it, one can't help thinking, "Good grief, that little piece of inconsequential word-play just cost me three hundred pounds."

Scene Three: at the gallery, night. Sound of London traffic outside

[*A sort of whisper*] This is usually the place where I feel completely safe. In the gallery. After hours. Shutters down. A few letters to shuffle about on the desk in an important manner [*paper*]. Outside, just a few fearfully well-dressed people darting past the window under black umbrellas, calling for taxis. Me cocooned in this lovely elegant space full of lovely elegant things, all mine, all worth thousands and thousands of pounds – which are currently, of course, out of harm's way in Montparnasse with the lovely Gideon, whose company I have sorely missed today, I must say, in my hour of need. The exquisite Honourable Araminta wafts ornamentally around the gallery on Tuesdays, of course, but since she's in direct line to inherit all of Wiltshire south of Devizes, she's hardly likely to be sympathetic to the fate of my little self-earned millions. [*Worried sigh*] I suppose it IS just the money Julian is after? Have I done enough to protect it? Why do I still feel as though I'm sitting on an unexploded bomb? That session with Dougie this afternoon was quite painful, but very interesting, because, of course, HE has an older brother who makes HIM feel insignificant, too! How could I have forgotten about Hamish? "But, Dougie," I said, "you're one of the best-paid lawyers in London." Since I was writing a very large first-consultation cheque to him at the time, I happened to know what I was talking about. "What does Hamish do?" I said, handing it over. "Is he Lord Chancellor or something?" And he said, as he smoothed the cheque and smiled at it in a loving kind of way, "Oh no, he runs golfing holidays in the Algarve." Astonishing. Of course, I nearly commented on the coincidence of the woman on the plane's husband being currently in the Algarve playing golf, but reconsidered just in time, and thereby saved myself – by retrospective calculation – the price of a fairly good ticket to the entire Ring Cycle at the Met.

[*Getting back to business; a sigh*] What a letter, though. I hope Gideon didn't look at it when he opened it. I'd hate him to know that anyone ever called me "Timmy". I showed it to Dougie, of course. In fact, I left it with him. He said there was something puzzling about it, and asked if I could find the envelope it came in, and I said I'd try. Gideon is terribly efficient, I said. He's probably shredded it. [*Not to Dougie*] I didn't tell Dougie, but the interesting thing, actually, is that Gideon also has an older brother who belittles HIM; yes! I suppose it's bound to be quite common, but it's quite a comfort none the less. In fact, when we happened to talk about our shared plight – it must have been just before I went to New York – Gideon said he had a theory that men with big brothers are a very particular brutalised personality type, and that they often have an unconscious bond with each other as a result. "Really?" I said. "Oh yes," he said. "Little brothers need to stick together," he said. "We're very easily taken advantage of." That's why he understood completely, you see, when I snapped into raise-the-drawbridge mode the moment I'd read that letter. I had only to call him and say, "Julian's coming! And he's calling himself head of the family!" for Gideon to say, "Mm, don't panic. I'll pack up the stock at the gallery and phone the bank! I can have everything in Paris by tomorrow afternoon!"

I'll go home soon. There's nothing more I can do here. I just keep thinking, if Julian's arriving on Thursday, he must already have set off. He's heading this way, and I'm rooted to the earth; it's like having the wrath of God galloping towards you; or Birnam Wood supernaturally on the march; or a hundred thousand orcs swarming across Mordor with battering rams and unbelievably long ladders. He'll be here the day after tomorrow. I'll have to congratulate him when he gets here. How clever to give me just enough notice to turn me into a nervous wreck.

Dougie thinks it was a bit strange to do that, though. [*Shrewd*] "Why did Julian forewarn you?" he said.

"Oh, he's a sadist," I said. "Julian won the amateur sadism trophy four years running at Marlborough."

Dougie looked unconvinced. He took a fork to a succulent Portuguese custard tart from Fortnum's, and masticated slowly. "Well, I think it's an odd thing to do. He's given you and your young Gideon two whole days to organise yourselves. You have to ask yourself, T.J.: what's the advantage to Julian of tipping you off?"

Scene Four: the Night Before the Big Day. Tim is at his desk at home; classical music in background; he has been drinking; he's slowed down a bit

[*A bit slurred already*] So. [*Drinks*] Three days ago, I was in New York. And I was so, so happy! [*Emotional*] I was on top of the world – at least, in the international art dealership sense of the thing. I had a lovely gallery waiting for me at home, a peerless Maffei under my arm, and I was in a yellow cab to Newark, the old wide rubber tyres bouncing over the bumps and potholes on the Manhattan cross-streets, the steam rising from the manhole covers; I could hear the honk of the early rush-hour traffic and the whistles and sirens of the traffic cops. [*Overcome; comically miserable*] I was somebody!

I haven't seen Gideon since Monday, because he's been overseeing a few complications in Paris; indeed, I've hardly spoken to him. [*Drinks*] So thank you, Julian, for that! [*Pours drink, with difficulty*] I don't know what plane Julian's on. I should have called the airlines, but – ugh, I'd need a [*looks round helplessly*] well, a phone and,

and, and a pencil and everything, and I'd have to GET UP, and [*he can't*] oof. Anyway, whatever time he comes, I'm ready. I've done everything. [*Drinks; he's beginning to slip into unconsciousness*] I'm as ready as I can be. This is a scorched-earth policy. Poor old Julian will be like Napoleon marching on Russia. Ha. There's nothing for him to get. I shall say, "I'm sorry. Reports of my success have been greatly exaggerated." [*On edge of sleep*] Just a load of scorched – scorched earth, nothing, nothing left for him to get ...

[*Asleep; heavy breathing*] The bastard.

Scene Five: in the gallery; traffic noises outside. Tim is hung over and trying to be brave while suffering

When Dougie called at ten about his cheque, I was shocked of course; but I have to admit that at some deep level I was not surprised, and I was even, perversely, relieved. It was as if all my life I'd been dutifully carrying a priceless Lalique vase around and then, suddenly, "Whoops!" it had fallen and smashed. "That cheque you gave me was a bad 'un, T.J.," he said. And I said, "Ah." And then I said, "Are you thinking what I'm thinking, Dougie?" And he said, "Well, I doubt it, because I'm thinking about a rather fine meringue I've just eaten. Whereas you, I suspect, are thinking, 'Ah, I don't know where Gideon is, and he's got the entire stock of my business, plus access to all my cash.'"

Of course, I called the bank, and when they said I had no access to the accounts any more, so they couldn't tell me why the cheque had bounced, I have to say, I laughed. Ha. Nervous laughter, I suppose. [*Laugh*] "Really?" I said. "Ha!" They said I'd signed over the company bank accounts to Gideon on Monday, by special arrangement, and I said, "I did do that, didn't I?" And they said, "Surely you have records, sir?" And I said, [*bluffing, worried*] "Yes! Yes, surely I do" – as I remembered proudly shredding the original forms on Gideon's brisk insistence, to prevent the rapacious Julian from discovering what I'd done. I said, "Er, oh, someone's just entered the gallery, may I phone you back later?" And they said I could do what I liked, I wasn't even a customer as far as they were officially aware.

[*Pause*] It was the wrong time of day to call Australia, but I did it anyway. I knew the number, even though I haven't called it for five years at least. It rang just twice and then – [*impersonates Julian; impatient*] "Do you know what bloody time it is?" It was Julian. At home in Sydney. In bed, asleep. Not on a plane. No macadamia nuts in his flight bag. No weird sheepskin artefacts. Just asleep, thousands, and thousands, and thousands of miles away. With his little brother a million miles from his thoughts. "It's Timmy," I said. [*Julian is pleased to hear from his brother*] "Timmy!" he said. "You in trouble? What's up? Oh no, [*laugh*] who do you want me to beat up for you this time?" It was a bit hard not to weep at that moment, I'll confess. It was a bit hard not to break down. "Julian," I said, as calmly as I could. "Um, you didn't write to me about a – er, an impending visit?" He said no, not at all. And sorry he hadn't e-mailed recently; business was fan-bloody-tastic. Come to think of it, he had called while I was in New York, he said, to ask about iPod and Region 1 DVD prices in London, and a posh bloke called Gideon had been quite friendly. "He seemed to be amused by the idea of me calling you Timmy," he said. "I got the feeling he was making a note. I hope you're not in love with that little tick." [*Pause*] Typical of Julian. Five years since I last spoke to him, and he hits the bull's eye first time. [*Faltering*] "Why on earth do you say that?" I said. "Sounded like a taker to me, Tim. Chaps like him can spot sad loveless quasi-homosexual losers like you a mile off." At which point Dougie appeared, at the door to the gallery, and I said I had to go. I'll call you back, Julian, I said. I've had a bit of bad news. Sorry I won't be seeing you. Bye.

Considering that I now had no immediate funds to pay him, Dougie was an absolute rock. "Do you actually know Gideon's in Paris?" Dougie asked, and I had to confess [*laugh*] I didn't know that, no. He could be anywhere. I cast my mind back to the scene in the gallery on Tuesday morning: to the boxes ready for shipping; the van outside; Gideon, in his blue suit, holding his passport in readiness; the peck on the cheek as he whispered, "It'll be all right, Teedge; I'll take care of everything." Those boxes. How do I know there was anything in them? I don't. My precious stock might have been sold already, or just hidden, at any time during my American sojourn – a trip, I now remembered, Gideon had quite vehemently encouraged me to take. On Tuesday morning, those forms from the bank were ready for me to sign, and the shredder hummed in anticipation. After that conversation about our unconscious bond, and how easily little brothers can be taken advantage of, Gideon knew that all he had to do was write that letter to me from Julian, and my automatic panic reaction would make me entrust my entire livelihood to my lovely assistant – an assistant I'd known only a few months, of course, and had never even kissed. [*Dougie*] "I knew it. This is your own writing paper, you idiot," said Dougie. I looked at it; it was. When he forged the letter from my brother, it seems, Gideon banked on me being so agitated by its contents that I wouldn't even spot that the stationery was from my own desk.

I kept thinking of Julian's first response when he heard my voice. "Oh no, who do you want me to beat up for you this time?" [*Emotional*] He meant that, you see. [*Laughs*] He's my big brother! Oh God. Now I come to think of it, he got one of his sadism awards for doing something to a chap who'd stolen my cricket bat. Imagine if he weren't there. I'd be on my own. No one else will ever offer to beat someone up for me, will they? On the other hand, of course, no one else will ever refer to me like that as a sad loveless quasi-homosexual loser, either. So I suppose it evens out.

[*To get his attention*] "T.J.!" Dougie said. Dougie was thinking what to do. Or possibly he was picturing a recently devoured choux bun, it's always a possibility. He asked me if I had any pictures of Gideon, and of course I didn't, because Gideon always said he was self-conscious about photographs, and refused to pose. Dougie said ah-ha! this showed just how deeply Gideon had laid his plans, and I said – and I'm afraid I may have been a little bit snappy, by now – [*impatient, voice rising*] that I really didn't see the point of anatomising all the cunning stages in Gideon's cunning, cunning, cunning plan. Gideon had merely deduced that my fatal weakness was my abnormally strong feelings of guilt, fear and resentment towards my older brother; it hardly required psychoanalytical genius, actually, to WORK THAT OUT.

[*Recovers from outburst*] "So," I said. "Why is everyone so keen on Region 1 DVDs all of a sudden, Dougie? What are they all talking about?"

Dougie said he didn't know. The modern world

was such a mystery to him, he was hoping soon to be appointed to the judiciary. "If it's any consolation, T.J.," he said. "I'd have done all the same things. Whenever Hamish calls up, I make the children tell him I've been kidnapped by Chechnyans. Marian says I've traumatised them, making up a story like that, because they're only eight and six, but I say what's the point in shielding them from the realities of life? By the way," he said. "Heard the good news?"

"What?" I said.

"Your namesake's doing very well at Wimbledon."

[*A sinking heart*] "What?" I said. "Oh no."

"Yes. Tim!" he said. "You know. Your namesake. They say he'll make the final this year, no problem. I've got debenture tickets tomorrow, would you like to come?"

And for the very first time, I felt like crying.

"What's wrong?" he said. "I don't understand."

[*Tearful*] "That's all I needed to hear, Dougie," I said. "Oh God, that's all I needed to hear."

The Wife

HENNY is a very nice person, good-humoured, self-effacing, a bit fussy; her problem is that she accepts criticism too readily.

Scene One: Henny has just got home from her work at a petting zoo. When she finds that husband Steve is not home yet, she is quite (guiltily) relieved, because she was worried about talking to him

I got this biscuit tin on the way home today, they were having a sale at the Trumpet Major tea rooms. It's more of a barrel really, and it took me ages to decide whether I could justify it because the old one's all right, just empty as it happens, because I finished off the bourbons last night while the news was on and gave it a nice wipe round, and you don't get rid of a biscuit tin just because it's empty, but on the other hand when does a biscuit tin wear out, it's hard to say isn't it, I've had mine for twenty-five years since I was married, and as Steve often points out it gets a lot of wear and tear our biscuit tin, what with Henny – that's me – having no willpower "What So Ever", well that's true of course, but they last for centuries so when can you buy a new one, and in the end I thought oh go mad, Henny, it's only two pounds fifty and if Steve really hates it you can take it to work, and charge the two pounds fifty to the Henny's Mistakes account which is definitely in credit at the moment because I paid in all my birthday money to cover that wall clock from Dorchester with the lemons on it that gave Steve the abdabs but they wouldn't take back.

[*Opens tin*] I think Steve will like this though. He might like it. I hope he likes it. I'm not sure I like it now actually. So, [*sound effects*] I'll just put all the new biscuits in it and hand it to him with our nine o'clock cuppa and see how he reacts. I mean, the woodland blackberry design is ever so inoffensive and I said to the woman in the shop, I don't want that one with the cuddly cute mice on it, I've learned my lesson, my husband can't stand cuddly cute mice crawling over teapots and aprons and chopping boards – especially not chopping boards. "I wouldn't want that one," he says, pointing at some mousy thing in a catalogue. "I know, Steve, I know," I say, but whatever I do I can't stop him saying, "I see enough mice at work, thank you, usually with their skins off," and I say, [*anxious, raised voice*] "I don't want to hear about it, Steve."

Funny he's not home yet. I'm three quarters of an hour late myself, which is almost unprecedented (!), but it's not like Steve to miss the 5.37. It's quite funny really; we moved down from Chessington to Thomas Hardy country – that's what they call it round here, like living in a book!

– but Steve's still a commuter, still does this job in the lab at Salisbury which is really hush-hush. I tell people he works for British Gas, which turned out to be quite a good idea because no one can ever think of an interesting follow-up question when you say British Gas, unless they want to complain about automatic switchboards. I say, "I know, I know, it's terrible, I know, push this, push that, yes, I know, please hold while we try to connect you, I know!" but it's better than arguing about animal rights, as I always get upset by that, obviously, when you consider how I personally quite like cute cuddly mice and everything, and when you consider my job! I tell Steve I don't like my job very much; I love it actually, but if Steve knew how much I loved it, he'd say it wasn't normal to be so enthusiastic, the place was unbalancing me, and start campaigning for me to leave. He hates to see me unbalanced, Steve. I told him I loved the civil service, you see, years ago. That's not normal, he said, and the next thing I knew, I'd left.

When we moved down here five years ago we didn't expect to find a job at all that would suit my meagre talents (!) – my "MTs" – but then this job came up at Bathsheba's, which, yes, IS a bit of a dramatic name for a petting zoo, but as Mr and Mrs Bryan say, everything else is named after Thomas Hardy things around here, so why shouldn't we be Bathsheba's Barn, with our Pair of Blue Eyes Teddy Bear Shop and a café called Far from the Madding Crowd? If Steve ever gets suspicious that I'm enjoying it, I invent something – tell him Mr Bryan is unnaturally close to the sheep, or the hamsters are smelly or something – and the bad news seems to cheer him up. Bathsheba's. It's a lovely name. Mr and Mrs Bryan aren't big readers, they don't pretend to be, but they got this big list of Thomas Hardy names from somewhere (I think everyone's got one), and we're working through it gradually and I think it's lovely. We've got a tiny goat called Eustacia and a goose called Jude. And you'd never think of names like that, would you? You'd call them Titch and Quackers or something. I did try to read one of Thomas Hardy's books recently, what Steve would call Overdoing It, but it was quite good, no really. Quite sad. Full of horrible ironic things that are somehow bound to happen; you see them coming, and you think, "Oh no, there's no escape from the very thing they were trying to avoid, no, no!" I got about halfway before I gave up. The thing is, it does put you off a bit when every time the name Tess comes up, you visualise a chicken.

Oh where's Steve? He knows I get worried if he's late. He ought to, we've been together since we were eighteen, it's our twenty-fifth anniversary in a couple of weeks, his mum's doing all the catering in case I couldn't cope with the worry, which is very nice of her, but at the same time, obviously, a bit worrying. Oh come on, Steve, I can't start cooking for tonight – can't start applying my meagre culinary talents, my MCTs! – till you get home and decide what you want. I'll start tucking into the biscuits in a minute! That biscuit barrel is lovely, anyway, there's no way Steve can say, "They saw you coming Henny" like he did with the lemon clock. We could use the old one for nuts and bolts or something. Not that we've got any nuts and bolts; we might have to buy some specially. Oh come on, Steve. He's an hour late! And now it's going to be awful when he gets home because whatever I say to him, even if I don't mention it, even if I say I did notice he was late but it didn't bother me, he'll say, "Don't go accusing me of anything, Henny; it's YOU that's not normal" and I won't be able to talk to him about Mr and Mrs Bryan offering me the job of manageress; I'll just have to go in to work tomorrow and say we talked about it, and Steve was all in favour but in the end I decided against it. [*Rehearsal*] We talked about it, Steve was all in favour. Oh come on, Steve! Come on. [*Opens tin*] I think I need a biscuit.

Scene Two; petting zoo noises

Well, it was a bit strange Steve not coming home at all last night, but I have to say, after the first three or four hours of worrying whether he'd been knocked down by a bus, or had forgotten his own name after a freak blow to the head, or the mice in the lab had finally ganged up on him and torn the living flesh from his bones with their sharp little teeth, I thought – possibly for the first time ever in my life – "There's a logical explanation for all this" and switched on the TV. It was very odd. Mad with worry for a few hours, ringing the hospitals, chewing my nails, and then, well, curled up with *Changing Rooms*. Where did Jude the goose get to? [*Goose honk*] He always looks depressed, this goose. [*Honk*] There he is! [*She imitates the goose noise*] Hello, Quackers! [*Honk, honk*] I know, it's terrible, poor you, eh? [*Honk*] Yes, yes. Poor Jude. Yes.

I even got out the reviled tapestry last night. I had a drink. I thought, "You're in shock, Henny. Go mad." I fell asleep on the sofa eating crisps watching something called *Never Mind the Buzzcocks*. The thing is, I don't know how I knew, but I did. I knew. He's not coming back. When I finally rang the police this morning, they said, "About twelve hours? Just overnight, madam? Give it another twenty-four," and instead of pleading with them to take me seriously, I said something really peculiar, what did I say? Hang on. They said, wait another twenty-four hours, madam ... [*Remembers*] And I said, [*cheerful*] "Right-oh."

Leaving the house was the most difficult thing about today. Every morning Steve and I leave the house together, you see, doing our checking in the kitchen: testing each appliance: taps off, cooker off, fridge shut, kettle unplugged; then door shut, light off, alarm set 1-9-7-6 (year we got married), double-lock the front door. Then we go in again. Taps off, cooker off, fridge shut, kettle unplugged; door shut, light off, alarm set 1-9-7-6, double-lock the front door. In again. Off, off, shut, unplugged; shut, off, 1-9-7-6, lock. Off, off, shut, unplugged, shut, off, 1-9-7-6, lock. We allow lots of time for this, because Steve's a stickler, and if he gets outside and can't remember whether the kettle was unplugged, we have to go back in and turn the alarm off and do it again, because he says he knows what I'm like, he doesn't want me fretting about it all day, imagining the house burning down.

So this morning, I didn't know what to do, with Steve not here. I looked round the kitchen and everything was – well, it was off. I mean, it was obvious everything was off. You can tell from looking whether things are off! So I set the alarm and shut the front door and locked it, and got in the car. And then I heard Steve in my head say, was the fridge shut? I pictured it; it was definitely shut. I mean, I hadn't tested it, pushed it, and said the word "Shut". But I still knew it wasn't open. So I started the car, and drove to work, and really didn't think about it until I'd just got past that exhaust centre place called Life's Little Ironies, and then I got this picture in my head [*fearful imaginings*] of Steve getting back from wherever he's gone, recovered his memory after a second blow to the head, patched the living flesh back on his cheeks after vanquishing the mice, and he goes in the kitchen expecting everything to be safe and orderly – and the door to the fridge is open. [*The horror!*] In fact it's swinging open and the food inside is all rotten and there's a pool of water on the floor. "Henny, how could you let this happen?" he yells, and he doesn't see the water in time, and he slips on it, and as he slips he grabs the kettle and it's not unplugged! And as he yanks it, the flex shorts at the plug and he dies in a shower of blue sparks and it's all my fault!

"Are you all right, Henny?" Mrs Bryan said. I was sitting in the car in Bathsheba's car park just outside the Gabriel Oak Experience – where twice a day the kiddies can take turns driving wooden stakes into the stomachs of pretend sheep blown up like balloons, apparently it was very memorable in the film, and we're quite proud of it because it combines good old violent country know-how with a nice thing from a book, and at the same time features the sound of escaping air, which is always so popular with children. [*Blows long expressive raspberry, to demonstrate*] Where was I? Oh yes. "Henny, are you all right?" Mrs Bryan says. "I need you to pump up the sheep when you're ready." And I make my decision. "Just got to pop home for something," and I drive all the way home and the fridge is shut and the kettle is unplugged, and I think I'm never, ever telling Steve about this, because he'll say I told you so and get me locked away. Still no sign of Steve, of course, not even [*wistfully*] fried to a crisp on the kitchen floor.

Scene Three: at home; music

Well, the police have been. I left it forty-eight hours in the end, so as not to look hysterical. Also, I lost track of the time watching *Pet Rescue*, which is great, I always thought it would be, Steve wouldn't let me watch it in case I got too involved. So I waited till that finished, and then they came, and now they've just gone. Two men and one woman. I'm glad there was a woman because she admired the biscuit tin. "So it's very unlike your husband to disappear like this?" they said, and I said, yes, totally. Detective Sergeant Law asked if I knew of any other relationships he had, and I said, "Well, there's his mother, I suppose I'd better tell her," and he said, delicately, he meant did Steve have a girlfriend or anything, and I burst out laughing. They all exchanged glances as if to say, "The wife is always the last to know" and DS Law said they would be looking into it anyway, so I said ha, good luck, and they exchanged glances again. They asked me to account for my movements on the day he disappeared and I think they were a bit surprised by some of the details but the woman police officer said she'd seen the film of *Far from the Madding Crowd* and the bit with the blown-up sheep was fantastic; she wouldn't mind having a go at that herself. They asked if he'd taken his passport, and I said of course he hadn't; he was only going to work. And then I looked in the drawer and actually it wasn't there, and mine wasn't either, and I started to think, "Oh spit, were we going on holiday and I've forgotten all about it?", but I didn't say that to the police because I'm sure normal people don't say things like that. So to change the subject I said, ooh Sergeant LAW, isn't it interesting the way people's surnames often fit their profession – all those TV gardeners called Flowerdew and Titchmarsh, and TV cooks called, and of course I couldn't think of one, so I said Rosemary Lemonsqueezer, and they just looked at me. DS Law asked about Steve. Did he have any history of mental illness? And I laughed again, and they said, "Do you have any reason not to love your husband, Mrs Williams?" And I said, "Of course not. I mean, leaving aside twenty-five years of marriage."

Scene Four: in the stationary car, with windscreen wipers going and heater fan

I rang Steve's Mum to tell her what had happened. She got hysterical at once, so I was glad I rang her from Bathsheba's. I said she ought to hold fire on the anniversary party stuff just in case Steve hadn't shown up by then. She couldn't seem to take it in; she kept asking, "But where's he gone?" and I kept having to explain that when someone's disappeared nobody knows where they've gone; that's the point of disappearing. In the end I said I'd ring her later. But it was obvious we should cancel the party: imagine we were passing round the mushroom vol au vents and the police turned up to say they'd found Steve's mutilated body or something. It would be like something out of a book. Or what if we turned it into a memorial tea, and he turned up? I sound like I don't care. I do care about what's happened to Steve; I'd hate him to be hurt or unhappy or dead. But after twenty-five years of living with him I just know he's all right. He's playing at something, and I just don't know what – perhaps he's trying to test me. Drive me over the edge with worry, like when we're halfway to Malaga and he'll say, "You OK now,

Henny?" and I say, "I'm all right if I don't look out of the window," and he says, "I've just thought, Henny, I don't want to worry you, but what if the regular milkman, who knows we're on holiday, is suddenly struck down with flu? And then there's a botched handover at the dairy and the replacement doesn't know we're on holiday, and leaves a pint of milk every day, and then the burglars spot all the bottles and they break in and take the telly?" Then we'll spend the rest of our holiday with me saying, "Look, I'll ring the dairy, I can easily get the number," and him saying to people, "Can you believe what my wife is worried about?" and them all looking at me and laughing.

Mr and Mrs Bryan called me in this afternoon from the Egdon Pleasure Park (the swings) and said the police had been round asking questions about me. "You realise we had to tell them everything we knew," said Mrs Bryan, bless her. She put a pay envelope on the desk, which was very odd because it was only the 17th, and said, "Would you like some time at home, dear? It must be hard to concentrate under all this strain." For a minute I couldn't think what strain she was referring to, and then I said, "No, I'm feeling fine, actually, apart from where that little boy at the Gabriel Oak Experience wielded his stake too far back and banged me in the eye." But Mr Bryan looked at the pay-packet, and folded his arms and didn't look at me. I realised they wanted me to go home, so I thanked them and took it, and got in the car and here I am. It's the first time I've been upset, to be honest. [*Sounds upset*] I feel like one of those sheep with all the air let out. It's not fair. All the time Steve was around I managed to keep my nice job; the minute he goes, and I'm free to enjoy it at last, my nice employers send me home.

Scene Five: home

I've been trying to read *Tess of the d'Urbervilles* again this afternoon, but it's a bit hard going. Not because of the story, actually, although I can't say I like it very much, the introduction says it's full of all these big dramatic ironies, and as Steve would say, "Well, that's not entertainment, is it?" No, it's the names. I mean, Angel Clare? Down the village you can get a very nice doggy perm and manicure at the Angel Clare. Why did the Bryans send me home? I can't believe they were so upset by the visit from the police, and anyway I don't see it's my fault that Steve's run off – or banged his head, or suffered the nasty living flesh thing. DS Law says now he's been gone four days they can check to see whether he's left the country, apparently they'll know later on today. I feel guilty that I don't miss Steve. I think that's why everyone's so suspicious, thinking I've bumped him off or something, because I've been so light-hearted. In fact, now I think of it, didn't Mrs Bryan come in yesterday when I was demonstrating the Gabriel Oak thing to the kiddies – stabbing that stake into that sheep – and really enjoying it? "Take that!" I was saying. [*Grunts of quite violent effort*] Uff! Oof! Uff! It was just after that she called me in and sent me home! Oh heavens! She thinks I stabbed Steve! Stabbed him until he flew around the room going [*blows raspberry*]. [*Serious*] It's funny, I've spent so much of my life worrying with Steve about things that don't happen, now something has really happened I feel I can't worry about it, as if I've done all the worrying already. It's only when I think, [*moved*] oh, Steve might never see the new biscuit tin –

I told DS Law, I thought I had to, that Steve did often say animal rights people might come after him for his job at the lab, and how he checked under the car for bombs. I felt very disloyal saying it; Steve feels so strongly that no one should know. But once I'd said it, and the DS was so surprised his jaw dropped, I started thinking, oh lumme, I must have made that up, it's very peculiar, isn't it? But the truth is, we've been checking under the car for years. Just common sense, Steve said. Self-protection. The threat of terrorism was just part of our lives – the house alarm, the mirrors on sticks for looking under the car, the perusal of the papers every day for stories of animal rights activists, the decision never to have children in case they were used as hostages or left orphaned. I mean, the very day Steve disappeared he'd cut a piece out of the *Times* about a senior research scientist in Denmark whose wife had been abducted. It does happen, I said. DS Law stopped writing it all down in his notebook, put down his pen, took a biscuit, and said the point is, though, Steve is not a senior research scientist, he's a lab technician. At the Fawley Research Centre, where he works, there are at least 150 people who are more likely to be targeted than Steve. And I said, [*brave laugh; it's a shock*] "I know that! Good heavens, I know that!"

I've been turning the place upside down looking for the passports, and of course I found stuff I've been hoarding – my degree certificate and this, my letter admitting me to the civil service. And suddenly, all these years of living like, like mice in the skirting board, just came over me in a wave, and I sat here, and I thought, [*quite upset; not angry, but sad*] spit, that was my life, Steve. What's happened to me? Twenty years ago I was on a fast track in the Home Office, and now I can't keep a job in a petting zoo. Now I agree with you and your mum about my "MTs" and having no willpower whatsoever, and I keep it a secret if I find joy in anything, so my husband can't say I'm unbalanced. No children. Didn't we work and worry strenuously to avoid children? And of course it never helped the mood exactly to have Steve breaking off to run downstairs to check the fridge was shut. And it was me who wasn't normal, apparently. I'm beginning to wonder what normal is, Steve. I'm beginning to think it's not really normal to sweep your front lawn for landmines.

Scene Six: home, happy music

It was just after DS Law left that it all happened. I was putting the biscuits away in the cupboard and I saw the old biscuit tin, and I thought, "Now, what am I going to use you for?", so I picked it up and opened it and inside there was this letter from Steve with my passport and quite a lot of cash in used notes. He had stuck a note saying "Don't Lose" on the passport and sealed up the letter in an envelope.

"To my wife," it said on the outside. "Urgent. Private. By hand." I turned over the envelope to open it and found on the back "Destroy After Reading". I opened it. I sat down. This had better be good, Steve, I thought. "Dear wife," it said. "This evening, June 15, I returned home from Fawley's at the usual time and found no sign of you. Alert to the Danish experience in this morning's *Times*, I naturally fear you have been abducted according to the same pattern; I also fear that if you have been abducted, they are really trying to get to me, so I am leaving immediately for Our Special Place, and hope you will join me there to prove my fears are groundless. However, if you do not follow me within three days I will conclude you are lost to me, even dead, and will remain abroad. I will place this letter in the biscuit tin as I know from twenty-five years' experience that reaching for the biscuit tin is always the first thing you do, my dear wife, having no willpower whatsoever. Buy your ticket with CASH. Check under the car VERY CAREFULLY. Steve. Above all, don't WORRY, I know what you're like."

I rang DS Law and told him. He said they'd just confirmed Steve had taken a flight to Malaga – our special place – but that otherwise they had no information. "You realise your husband is insanely paranoid?" DS Law said. I asked him, is it insanely paranoid not to have children because you're afraid they'll be used at some later date as hostages – and he said yes, that was more or less a definition of insanely paranoid, in his opinion. "You seem to have missed his three-day deadline," he said. And I said, [*almost stunned; can't believe her luck*] "Yes, that's my reward for going mad and buying a new biscuit tin." Then I counted the cash, which was over three thousand pounds, and rang Mrs Bryan with the good news. She said I could start back tomorrow, and the job of manageress was still open if I wanted it. She also said the goats had missed me, which I think was her way of apologising for thinking I'd stabbed my husband to death.

It said on the news, by the way, that the Danish woman hadn't been kidnapped after all! The lovely Elsa had run off with her younger lover and hadn't known how to mention it. The adulterous carefree pair were last seen, funnily enough, in Malaga.

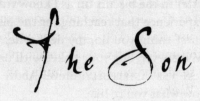

The Son

MARK *is a casual, laid-back and rather shallow character
who takes everything in his stride. He has been a staff
photographer on a newspaper for twenty years. He loves
his car and is proud of all the equipment, but isn't much
bothered about his art.*

*Scene One: driving. He's humming while driving, and interrupts
himself to comment on the traffic*

All right, mate, you go. No, YOU go. Right-o. [*Hums. Reads
sign*] Bexleyheath, right. What's the time? Oh. Cushti.
Just me on this job today. No poncey lady feature writer
saying, "Oh take no notice of Mark, he's just the photographer." No, this is more like it. Simple news desk job.
[*Happy sigh; contented with the normal routine of his life*] Find
house, ring doorbell, "Hello, Mr Watts, you're some sort
of news story I understand, no don't bother telling me

about it, I'm not remotely interested, yes, hello, Mrs Watts, well I wouldn't say no, two sugars, can I move this lamp, is that a jaffa cake, ta very much, does that window open, can I use this socket, flash bang wallop, back in the car, laptop, mobile, bit of quick image manipulation, send, send, send, and back to me mum's in Fulham in time for *The Weakest Link*.

[*Manoeuvring*] Bexleyheath. [*Remembering instructions*] Left at the roundabout. [*Manoeuvres*] Straight on for three miles. [*Sigh*]

So, not like yesterday, that's what I'm saying. Yesterday was well weird. I said to Kip on the picture desk, "Kippo, mate, you know me, I'm not into the arty stuff. I didn't sign up for that. I'm more of what you might call an all-rounder, only with a particular aptitude for prison vans. That's right, I'm a legend outside the law courts. The only snapper who can ALWAYS get a shot through the window of a moving black maria. And that's not fluke. David Beckham practises free kicks round the wall. I practise black maria technique. You've got to jump EXACTLY the right height, see, at EXACTLY the right moment, holding the camera above your head at EXACTLY the right angle." Kippo looks at me. "Straight up?" he says. And I say, [*confidential, as if giving away his secret*] "Well, yeah, fairly straight up, but with a crucial last-minute kick in the direction of travel."

"Well, doing a few portraits won't kill you," he said. [*Kippo doesn't understand it himself*] "Seven mediums," he said. "It's for the magazine. Juliet Frampton's doing seven interviews, and they want a pic for each one. Hang on, I'll ring the mag." He reached for the phone while I just stood there, rolling my eyes and hoping he'd suddenly think of someone better suited to the job. "David?" he said. "Jimmy Kipling, picture desk. These seven mediums of Juliet's. Yeah, I got your list of addresses. Yeah, got a great bloke here. Mark King, you know him? Good. You'll have seen loads of his stuff, he's been on the paper for, what?" [*He's asking Mark; Mark has to think about it; a bit astonished*] "Twenty years," I said. "Twenty-five years," he said. "What? [*Lying*] Yeah, Marko's VERY sensitive, yeah. Very. Very, what's the word – [*a prompt from the mag man*] what? Oh yes, that's right, intuitive, yes. And if you need any specialist jumping done at the same time, incidentally, he's your man. Anyway, just one question. This word mediums. Shouldn't that be media? Oh. Coz I've been trying to visualise. What's a medium then? Oh. Oh, I see, I'll call you back, then, cheers." He turns to me. "Er, Marko, you're going to do seven very sensitive and intuitive portrait photographs of psychics. In between your normal jobs, of course. And the first one's this afternoon in Hackney."

I gave him one of my looks. Although I don't know why I bothered because my looks have never had an effect on anyone. At home, when I was little, I'd do one of my looks and everyone else would laugh like drains. [*A happy memory; he loved his dad*] My dad used to fall off his chair, the bastard. "Jill'd be good for this, Kippo," I said. "Or even the Giant Padster, if you can spare him from Cheltenham. I mean, seen one photo finish, you've seen 'em all." Kippo looked at the list. "Tell you what, one of these is in Middlesbrough next Tuesday. You could catch the Lazio second-leg at the Riverside. Johnners could get you in. He might even get you an armband." Well, that was a bit of a decider. "I'll pack a warm jacket," I said. "Good man," said Kippo. "Good man."

[*More driving required, slowing down*] Hang on, left here.

Sutherland Road. That's it. Should be down on the right. [*Reading house numbers*] Sixty-eight. Ninety. Hundred and six. Hundred and ten. Hundred and twenty. [*Stops the car*] Here we are, then. Number one-four-four. And what's the time? Twenty past? Great. [*Switches off engine*] Oof. I've even got a few minutes to spare.

So anyway, off I went to Hackney yesterday afternoon, to meet Juliet and our first medium, who was this very unassuming old bloke in a nice cardigan, and I whispered to Juliet as we looked round, "Not a lot of cash in this psychic malarkey, then?", which she ignored because she's a bit stuck-up, being a) from Features, b) married to Brian Frampton, the deputy editor, and c) runner-up in 1997 for Broadsheet Stuck-up Feature Writer of the Year. Anyway, the bloke's name was Lister. Mister Lister. He made us a cup of coffee and he was obviously quite nervous, coz his hands were shaking, but Juliet didn't notice. What she did notice straight away, however, was that the poor old geezer couldn't get the hang of who was in charge between us. He kept saying things like, "And would the, er, lady like sugar?" and all the while addressing me instead of her, even though I made a big show of deferring to Juliet. "Oh, Juliet's the boss," I kept saying. "She's the words and I'm just the pictures." In the end, she said, rather pointedly, "Would it be all right for Mark to scout for a good place for the photographs?" And Mister Lister looked confused but said all right.

It was a sad old house, really. Old bloke on his own. It felt like he'd been on his own for about thirty years. Pictures of his wife on the walls, the last dating from around 1970. Framed drawings in pastel of Arabs and Chinese – it all felt quite normal to me, to be honest, coz there was quite a bit of spiritualism in my dad's family; my granddad had a spirit guide called Abdul and my Auntie Madge had one called Mister Chin. In fact, Mister Lister had a framed cartoon at the top of the stairs that would have amused that lot. There was this medium gazing into a crystal ball and saying, [*he's amused by this*] "Well, Mr So-and-so, I'm afraid I can't contact your late aunt, but there's a horse here who'd like to say hello."

[*The thing is, Mark IS intuitive; he just doesn't know it*] This bloke Mister Lister could have been my granddad. His house had the same smell, you know, of old lino and hard cheese, and wet wool and calamine lotion. I took a dozen shots or so, and then [*he shivers*] I suddenly thought, "I hope this feature isn't going to be one of Juliet Frampton's famous chainsaw massacres, coz he doesn't deserve that." So I went back downstairs and knocked lightly on the open door to the living room and found Juliet and Mister Lister both looking a bit – well, uncomfortable. I sensed at once there had not been a meeting of minds.

"So would you let me say it's about being OPEN?" she said, with pen poised above notebook. He winced and shook his head. Evidently she was pressing Mister Lister to unlock the secret of his craft, and he wasn't having any of it.

I took a couple of discreet shots from the doorway, and Mister Lister looked up. [*Relief*] "Oh, but here's our friend back at last! Young man, I've got a message for you!"

[*Beat*] I laughed. "Oh, I don't think so."

Juliet was pursing her lips, she was well wound up, so I grabbed a quick couple of shots of her to wind her up even more. It had exactly the desired effect. "Mark!" she said. "Could you please not interrupt?"

"Oh but this isn't an interruption, dear," said Mister

Lister. "The spirits don't interrupt us. We interrupt THEM. And there is someone here who would very much like to say something to Mark."

[*Laugh*] "Is it a horse wanting to say hello?" I said.

Mister Lister laughed, and Juliet looked so confused that I snatched another shot of her. It was a classic, actually. I'm going to blow it up and use it as a screensaver. Evidently not only was this assignment foisted on her, you see, but it turns out, if she hadn't been here, she could have been at the Hyatt Regency in Portman Square gazing into the eyes of Jude Law over a cup of steaming Lapsang.

But back with this message. "It's a very practical message," Mister Lister said. "Your dad is unusually straightforward, isn't he?"

[*Cheerful, affectionate memory*] "Yes, he is. I mean, he was."

"Well. He says, Marky, Marky, you've got a head like a sieve."

I shrugged and laughed. It was true. Good old Dad.

"He says you forgot your dry-cleaning ticket for those combats of yours, didn't you?"

I rolled my eyes at Juliet. Tsk!

"Well, he says luckily your mum will remember it in about ten minutes' time, just before the shop closes, so you'll still have your outfit for tonight."

They both looked at me for my reaction.

"Ha!" I said.

"So that message does mean something to you?" said Mister Lister. He seemed anxious, I don't know why.

[*Not overwhelmed at all; as if it's quite normal*] "Oh yeah. Totally. Good old Dad."

Juliet seemed to think this wasn't an adequate reaction.

"Mark, are you saying that sounded like a message from your father WHO IS DEAD?"

[*A shrug; what of it?*] "Yeah?"

She looked completely astonished. She also had the rather worrying look of someone whose brain mechanism is suddenly whirring very, very quickly.

"Any message for your father in return?" said Mister Lister.

"Oh. Oh OK. Could you say thanks a bunch, Dad? Blimey, I'd be lost without those combats."

Scene Two: at home, at his computer, which hums. He's looking at the pics

What a brilliant tool Photoshop is. [*Keypad and mouse noises*] That's a nice one. Hello, Mister Lister! Ooh, that's a very nice mauve cardigan shot, if I say so myself. I'll have that. [*Tap. Mouse*] And enlarge. [*Tap. Mouse*] Lovely. Of course, this is the point in the movie when the guy says, "Hold it! What's this strange shining mark to the right of Mister Lister's head? Jeepers, I'd better call an archbishop!" Whereas in fact there IS a spooky light area, obviously, in every single one of these shots, but if I just – [*mouse clicks and scrolls*] airbrush it – [*more clicks*] like this – [*more clicks*] and that – [*more clicks*] Hey presto. The telltale spooky shining mark has gone!

I went to see Kippo straight after the job yesterday. Went back to the office and asked him to take me off the mediums. I mean, it's not that I'm not interested. It was really nice hearing from my dad like that. I told Mum about it, and she said, well, if you get him again, could you please ask him what he did with the key to the coal-shed because we'll have to break the door down sooner or later. No, the problem was working with Jules. She called me up when I was driving back and said, all urgently, "Look, Mark, we have to talk –" And the trouble was, I know her well enough to know where that was leading. I mean, nothing romantic, nothing like that. When our little thing finished a year or two ago, we agreed – well, we agreed we'd been lucky to get away with it, so leave it at that. It wasn't as if our paths would ever cross professionally, what with me lurking round the Old Bailey with the other snappers doing my impersonation of a salmon leaping upstream, and her in hotel lobbies hypocritically sucking up to film idols. I don't think either of us minded very much about splitting. We did quite suit each other, though. I mean, you know. For a woman, she's not exactly deep.

How we managed to keep it totally quiet I don't know, but we did. Amazing. I mean, it was obvious yesterday that Kippo had no idea, for a start, and Kippo is the biggest gosser on the staff; it was him that first sussed the two-jacket ploy that old sports editor invented twenty years ago: leaving the spare jacket on the back of the chair mid-morning as if he'd just popped to the canteen for a packet of fruit gums, and then legging it to the Waldorf to meet that woman from the Football Association. Anyway, the point is, I couldn't tell Kippo the real reason I didn't want to do the job, could I? So I told him about my dad's message and how it had turned out to be uncannily completely accurate.

"You see?" I said. "I didn't sign up to be a press photographer so that I could have supernatural experiences, Kippo. I did it for the cash and the chicks and the Saab and for the incredibly long lenses, and for a nickname ending in 'o'."

Kippo thought about it. He didn't look convinced. "Well, if your dead father is going to send you messages, Marko, it would be great for the piece."

[*Groan*] I'd been really hoping he wouldn't say that. It was exactly what Jules had said when she phoned me up. People who work on newspapers always just want the STORY; it's a bit depressing, if you ask me. "We can USE your dad, if he's going to come through like this!" she said. "I could interview him from beyond the grave!" I could see her thinking, Broadsheet Stuck-up Feature Writer of the Year 2005, here I come.

"Kippo!" I said.

"I think you should do the two on Wednesday –"

"TWO?" I said.

"Do the two on Wednesday and see what happens, Marko. That dry-cleaning ticket thing was obviously just a way of convincing you that it was really him."

I didn't say anything. It had never occurred to me that it wasn't really Dad. Why on earth would Mister Lister pretend he had a message from my dad?

"You got on well with your dad, didn't you, Marko?"

"Well, my dad got on with everybody. He was a nice bloke."

"You think everyone's a nice bloke."

His phone rang.

"Juliet Frampton isn't," I muttered, darkly.

And he laughed and said, "Yeah, but that didn't stop you banging her for two years twice a week at that flat in Broadwick Street, did it? No such thing as a secret, Marko. Hello, picture desk."

Scene Three: in the car again, but stationary with the windscreen wipers going

[*Sigh; shiver*] I'm beginning to feel like that bloke in *Randall and Hopkirk (Deceased)*. Using my gigantic powers of deduction, I think I must be Randall. Oh come on, Juliet. If I've got to drive you back into town, you might get a move on! Look at that rain! Tell you what, these jeans are soaked from lying on that grass to get the shot through the patio doors.

I'd better not mention *Randall and Hopkirk* to Juliet. But it's that TV thing from the sixties with the two detectives where one of them dies and then comes back to help in the investigations. They remade it recently with Vic Reeves. The point is, the dead one is invisible to everyone except his old partner, so he can shout helpful things like, "He's behind you, Jeff!" and, "He's got a gun, Jeff!" And sometimes, if he blows really, really hard, he can make a curtain billow or a candle go out. It's quite entertaining, but as my dad used to say when we watched the re-runs, it's hardly an ennobling vision of the afterlife. I mean, in the past, people dreaded death for respectable reasons like hell and purgatory, where at least there was an element of personal improvement involved. You were kind of purified in the flames. Whereas now – well. Even more reason to dread death if all you do afterwards is hang around shouting, "You're about to fall in a hole! Can you hear me? You're about to fall in a – You see? You fell in a hole!"

Sorry, it's been a strange day. These jeans are really sticking to me now. And Jules is being AWFUL. She rang me again last night, with a plan this time, about how we could sort of trap my dad into becoming the focus of this piece of hers. "It could be like a Day in the Life!" she said. "Only with the difference that he's not alive!" I thought quickly about what to say. I didn't come up with much. "You still fancy me, don't you, Jules?" I said. And she said, "What's that got to do with anything?" And I said, "I knew it!" But she wasn't so easily sidetracked, unfortunately. She was beginning to see my dad as her key to fame. Any objections on my part wouldn't really bother her. So when we went into the house and met these two, well, you could only call them witch-ladies, I made a point of going straight out into the garden, where I took a few lying-down shots of the house with a yellow filter to make the sky look scary. But I didn't get away with it for long. I was just texting Kippo a lengthy joke about a bloke whose car breaks down in the Arctic Circle when one of the witch-ladies came out and said I had to join them at once. I'd been there for all of eight minutes, and she and her friend had been bombarded with messages for me; [*falsetto*] "Like psychic spam!" she said. "Ah," I said.

Jules was looking all expectant when I got back in, although she curled her lip a bit at the wet trousers. "Mark and I are developing an interesting relationship," she trilled. "A bit like Salieri and Mozart. Mark is the one singled out for all this supernatural attention, you see, but he doesn't appreciate how special it is. Whereas I understand its importance, and all I can do is watch." They looked baffled. "Plus I think she wants to kill me," I said.

So, here were the messages I got from my dad. I can hardly wait to hear what Jules thought of them all.

One. Someone is breaking into your car. (This was true. I ran outside and chased them off.)

Two. The Chelsea starting line-up tonight will be the first ever premiership side to contain no English players.

Three. Being dead is a bit boring, so remember to take multivitamins.

Four. Why do you keep airbrushing me out of all your pictures?

Five. There never was a key to the coal-shed. Just kick it on the side and the door springs open.

Six. You're right, son. She does still fancy you.

Oh God.

Scene Four: driving back from Middlesbrough

Go on, then, mate, overtake, that's right. Little wave wouldn't hurt, would it? Good.

[*Sigh*] We did our last one today. Middlesbrough. There were supposed to be three more; we were supposed to be heading north tomorrow, but I'm going home. Shame about the match at the Riverside. Johnners had not only got me an armband, he'd got me a kip for the night and all.

We had to see this woman today, you see, Jane Starling, her name is, she helps the police with their inquiries and has a framed letter on the mantelpiece from the Strathclyde Constabulary acknowledging her assistance in finding bodies and weapons and caches of gold bullion. And she wasn't a bit like the others; she was really abrupt and businesslike. She was even quite hostile when we arrived. Especially towards me. [*Geordie accent*] "I don't want HIM in here, pet," she said, without even looking at me properly. "He's draining all me psychic energy and he's hardly got his foot through the front door, like." Of course, I said, [*cheerful; relieved*] "Okey dokey; your house!" and was halfway back to the car, but Jules dragged me back in, saying, "Oh, Mark has that effect on everyone! [*Laugh*] Half an hour in his company and most people lose the will to live!"

Hang on, where are we? Junction 24. Bloody hell, that's not far. I'll have to take a rest in a minute. I'll be doing the rest of this in the dark as it is.

Anyway, where was I? Oh yes. I reckon the problem with this Jane Starling woman is that nobody believes in her in the normal run of her life. They think she's some kind of fraud. Hence the peculiar aggression at the outset.

"Remember the Pammy Babcock case?"

"No."

"Well, it was me who found that hairbrush!" [*He doesn't react*]

"Remember the Glasgow bullion robbery?"

"Er, no."

"It was me who told them to focus on a grey van with the number seventeen on the licence plate." It was a bit tiring, all this, and I could see Jules was starting to get fed up with her, so she said, very carefully, "Mrs Starling, I haven't come here to judge you in any way, or test you. I just want to talk to you about your gift. And if you have any messages for either of us, that would be marvellous. We have had a few messages recently from Mark's dad, but they've been a bit – well, to be honest, they've been a bit banal."

Mrs Starling shrugged. Since most of the messages she received were about hairbrushes and licence plates, she was hardly likely to be sympathetic. But Jules was insistent. I was sitting next to her on the sofa. "If you manage to speak to Mark's dad first," said Jules, "could you impress on him that what we'd really like –" I don't know where the "we" came from, but anyway – "what we'd really like is something a bit less to do with, well, sport, or missing keys, or cleaning tickets, that sort of thing."

"Right, pet," said Mrs Starling, but she didn't look happy.

I grabbed a couple of shots of the room while we were waiting.

[*Long pause*] "Anything?" Jules said.

I took some more shots.

[*Long pause*] "Anything yet?"

"Well – no." [*Pause*] "Er –"

[*Breathless*] "Yes?" Jules was so excited she dug her nails into my knee.

"I'm not sure. It's to do with the new *Doctor Who*, like."

Jules thumped my knee with her fist. "No!" she said. "Ow!" I said.

"Right," said Mrs Starling.

Jules glared at me as if all this was my fault. I just shrugged. I really wanted to hear the *Doctor Who* news. In fact, I was just about to stop all this and ask Mrs Starling to go back a bit, when she gave up anyway.

"It's no good, pet. All I can get is some stuff about Christopher Eccleston, the winner of the 3.30 at Doncaster, a reminder that the clocks go forward at the weekend, and the words, 'He's behind you, Jeff!', which he says you'll understand."

Jules nearly screamed, but I took a more rational position. I looked at the clock. It was just after three. "It wasn't Laughing Dingo, was it? In the 3.30?"

"It was, pet. How did you know that?"

"Well, he was rubbish last time out, so that would be very interesting, you see."

Jules said, "Please shut up, Mark. [*Gritted teeth*] Anything else, Mrs Starling?"

[*Pause*] "Oh yes. He's fifteen to one, like!"

"No, I mean, anything else besides the racing tip."

"Oh. Well, no."

And then the phone rang and Mrs Starling positively shot out of her chair to answer it. We heard her in the hall. [*Relief*] "Chief Inspector!" she said. "You've no idea how pleased I am to hear from you!"

Jules and I sat there together in silence. I knew she was angry with my dad, but I didn't see what I could do about it. I wondered whether to tell her the joke about the man in the Arctic with the Inuit AA, but decided to carry on texting it to Kippo instead. In the hall, Mrs Starling was saying things like, "HOW many fingers did you say, Inspector? Mm, well, I've never worked with less than the full hand, but there's a first time for everything!" In the end, of course, just as I sent my text to London, Jules spoke first.

"You know those messages at the witch-ladies', Mark? What did your dad mean about you airbrushing your pictures?"

I'd been hoping she hadn't remembered that. I got the big Nikon out of the bag and held it up for her to see the screen on the back. [*Matter-of-fact*] "I have to get rid of these shiny lights all the time, that's all." I brought up one of the Mister Lister pictures and pointed to the corner. A spot of silvery light. "There," I said. I scrolled through half a dozen more. "See? It's there. There. There. Bit of a nuisance, that's all." I looked at Jules. I knew it: she was impressed.

"This couldn't be a defect in the camera?" she said.

"No," I said. "It's been in every picture I've taken, with every camera I've used, for the past ten years."

"What, even in news pictures?"

"Yeah. But it's quite easy to blank it out."

"We could print these, Mark!"

"Nah," I said.

"Why not?"

"Because people would assume I'd tampered with them, Jules. The way I tamper with them already."

Oh good. Services two miles.

So what happened then? Oh yeah. Mrs Starling came back with a tray of tea. She'd been really cheered up by the call from the plod. "Sorry I couldn't help much, pet," she said. "Funny how things are. Ask me to locate a headless corpse in Grimsby, like, and I'm off like a greased whippet. Wagon Wheel, anyone?"

She put down the tea and munchies, and then went back in the hall, found her purse and put her coat on. It was ten past three. She was evidently heading for the bookies, and I didn't blame her.

"I've got another message from your dad," she said. "He's a bit worried, pet. He says to ask, you don't think he's a bit SHALLOW, do you?"

"Course not," I said. "Er – you couldn't, if you're going to the bookies?" I reached in my wallet and pulled out a fifty. She took it.

"Right, pet. Fifty on the nose. You won't regret it, like. Anyway, the thing is, pet, he says other spirits send better messages than this, don't they, about love and stuff. 'I'm so proud of you, son,' that kind of thing. 'I never told you enough when I was alive!' He doesn't want you to feel left out. He's worried you'll think he's not as deep as the other dads."

"But I know he loves me," I said. "I know he's proud of me. He did tell me enough when he was alive. No, tell him I've never had a minute's doubt in my whole life, and I'm forty-two. Besides, what's wrong with shallow? I'm shallow, Jules is shallow; you're a bit shallow yourself, Mrs Starling; it's what keeps us cheerful. Why should I want Dad to be any different just because he's dead?"

She put her arm round me and kissed me on the head. "You're a good son, pet. You're your father's son. And I'll be back at about twenty to four with the winnings!"

We heard the front door slam and then we saw her sprint past the window with a determined look on her face. Jules turned off her tape recorder and put her notebook away. My phone beeped. It was probably Kippo. I decided to ignore it. Jules and I might be having a togetherness moment.

[*Gentle*] "Have you really always known your dad loved you, Mark?"

"Oh yeah."

I put my arm round her. I know I'm lucky. I felt I should say something sort-of profound and reassuring.

"So, there's this bloke driving across the Arctic when his car breaks down."

"Heard it," she said.

I nestled closer to her. [*Soft*] "Jules," I said. "When I said you were shallow just now, I was only being rhetorical, you know that, don't you?"

"Look, whatever your dad says, I don't still fancy you, Mark," she said.

So I said, [*taking arm away; little sigh*] "Oh. All right, then. Fair enough."

The Mother

JANEY is bright, posh Scottish, brittle.

Scene One: at a health spa. Sounds of swimming pool

"You have the skin of a thirty-year-old, Mrs Phipps," Maureen said to me this morning. And I said to her, "You're heading for a very large gratuity, Maureen, if you keep saying things like that." Whether she heard me I don't know. I was lying on her massage bench at the time with my face pressed through the face-hole-thing, and Maureen was putting a lot of puff and effort into shoving all the flesh on my back up to my neck – I suppose there's a chance that one of these days it will stay there. I have to say I smiled to myself – a bit reckless, I know, when you consider the wear and tear on the facial lines. But a thirty-year-old! What would Sasha say? Sasha being twenty-one, that would have me giving birth to her at the age of [*thinks about it*] … nine! Eight? Nine. I was so bucked up. I mean, my hands are good for my age. And I've made a point of never plucking above the lip, which Maureen agreed will certainly pay dividends in the long run. The only thing that spoiled it was at the end, when I was just getting back into the fluffy white bathrobe and slippers and Maureen said, "So. Mrs Phipps. How do you find your skin?" Well, I didn't know what to say. HOW DO YOU FIND YOUR SKIN? "What a strange question," I said. "Everywhere I look on my body, Maureen, it's there."

How I love dear old Woodlands. This is my fifth time. Of course I get the detox headaches, but somehow I always go home a couple of pounds lighter, rested, and with a sort of glow. I finally had my colours done yesterday – I'm a spring person, which came as no surprise. I should wear greens, yellows, peach, pink, lilac. "There's a very famous spring person, when you think about it, Mrs Phipps," the woman said. So I thought about it. Greens, yellows, pinks. "Elton John?" I said. "The Queen," she said. And it was one of those lovely moments when everything falls into place. Anyway, before that I had the manicure, the pedicure, the astringent neck poultice, the deep sonar navel cleansing, the organza scrub and the all-body Bering Straits seaweed. Oh, and the long-distance hosing, which was a bit like finding yourself in the path of a water cannon, actually, but they promise is fantastically good for the flabby bit under the arm, although I read somewhere in a magazine that if you TALK to the flabby bit under the arm, sit it down with a cup of coffee and really explain to it that it's nothing personal, it's just not welcome, there's a real possibility it will give up and throw in the towel. The colours lady – whose name is Ros, and who I did think might have been a man dressed up, actually, monarchist or not – anyway, Ros says when I get home I must simply throw away all my wintry blacks and purples, autumny browns and tans, and summery [*thinks*] ... summery whatever they were. According to Ros I have been locked in an unconscious pigmentation tussle with my own wardrobe! For years! And I always assumed the enemy was – within.

I phoned Sasha just before the optional introduction-to-yoga class, where a chap called Gerald in lemon socks asked us brightly what we thought of when we heard the word "spirit", and I suppose I was still thinking what's wrong with Sasha, a girl who since puberty has had absolutely no spirit at all. "Anyone?" he said, looking round. "Janey?" He pointed a finger at me, revolver style, and pulled the imaginary trigger. I went all hot. People were looking.

"Me?" I said.

"Yes, Janey. Tell us what you think of when you hear the word spirit."

"Spunk," I said. A pained expression flashed across his face as if he were chewing a bee, so it obviously wasn't the right answer, and he turned to the Irish woman with the gold jewellery and the soaraway pashmina import business.

"Well, I wasn't THINKING of spunk," he said. "But yes, yes, I think I –"

"Get up and go," I explained.

"Thank you, Janey," he said.

"Nerve, guts, va-va-voom," I said.

"Yes, I see where you're going with that, Janey," he smiled. "Now, Dervla. What do you think of when you hear the word ... spirit?" She fiddled with the end of her apricot pashmina.

"Would you be thinking of the *Blair Witch Project* at all?" she said. At which point Gerald gave up on the interactive experiment and pushed on with his flip-chart. Tried to sell us a yoga holiday. He gave me his card later, when I let him buy me a low-calorie elderflower presse with no strings attached. He had a nice nose. Lovely hair. But a man with lemon socks? I couldn't. I thought about it quite deeply afterwards, and I – just – couldn't.

Anyway, when I phoned Sasha, the Rotter was there in the background, I could hear him. "Are you suffering to be beautiful then?" she asked, in her usual hurtful way. I told her that actually the deep sonar navel thing wasn't at all pleasant, the boom echoed inside for hours and they hand you the fluff afterwards in a little plastic tub, several inches of it, so I still felt a bit sick, and then happened to mention that the masseuse said I had the skin of a thirty-year-old. Why do I never learn? Sasha covered the receiver and said something to the Rotter – only she doesn't call him the Rotter, she calls him Mike. The Rotter shouted loud enough for me to hear, "Wait till the thirty-year-old finds out!" And Sasha laughed. She doesn't want me to be happy. She is the centre of my world, the core of my being, the offspring of my youth – although I wasn't nine, obviously, when I had her, I was twenty-two. How can I bear it that she never, ever wants me to be happy?

Scene Two: evening, at home. TV in background. She is deflated

It was sad getting back to the house. I wonder if I should buy some humidifiers – this dead atmosphere can't be good for the skin. I mentioned it to Sasha once, but she said it was me. "What, my imagination?" I said. And she said, "No, it's you that causes the dead atmosphere."

Sasha did go to university for a while. Her father insisted on it, suddenly taking an interest after fifteen years. He wanted her to go to Oxbridge, which I found out isn't even a place, so that shows what he knows about it, and I said Bath had some nice shops, so she went there. She's a very very clever girl but I was right, she's got no spunk. I've heard her tell people she came home because I blackmailed her emotionally, which I most certainly did not. I don't even know what it means. But that's her story. "You threatened to top yourself, so I came home," she says, in the same dull flat way she says everything. If the house was on fire, she'd say, "You'd better call the fire brigade" in the same depressed way other people say "I've got that rash back between my toes." It's tremendously difficult to enthuse or even engage Sasha. "What now?" she says. "Oh, what now?" I mean, this is just an example, but say I tell her I'm desperately in love with a new man – but what shall I do, he's married! [*Pause for effect*] I say it's so ghastly he never calls. [*Pause*] "And what if I'm pregnant, Sasha! I'm so happy, I'm so worried, there's a higher chance of Down's syndrome at my age, shall I book the test?" [*Pause; then angry*] Doesn't she care? What's the point of sharing information with someone you love if they don't take it on board? When I got home last night, she pointedly didn't even ask how Woodlands had been so I just told her. "Darling," I said, "I feel so happy and relaxed." She was putting the kettle on, with her back to me. "It'll pass," she said. It'll pass. To think I was going to show her the little plastic pot with the fluff. And then I don't know, it all went wrong. I said, "I hope you're coming to my birthday dinner on Friday." And she said, "Can Mike come?" And when I hesitated, she said, "Well, who else will be there? Last time I counted, you didn't have a single friend." So I said people with fat faces shouldn't wear V-necks, and she walked out of the kitchen, walked out and left me sitting there.

But what is it to be a mother? It is a one-way street. If I've learned nothing else, it's that you must pour yourself, all your love, in your child's direction and expect nothing in return. You must even accept the Rotter without complaint, who now appears to have moved in, to judge by the number of sheepskin jackets hanging in the hall and the way his car battery is being recharged in the dining room. It was the stress of the Rotter that drove me to Woodlands. She first brought him home about a month ago, a photographer for the glossy magazine she works on, whatever it is, something to do with having nice curtains. Her father got her the job, so we have him to thank for the Rotter as well. Anyway, Mike's about thirty, dark, divorced, ambitious, hair stuck up like an urchin, eyes of caddish blue. And it's such a disappointment, to see how he just has to flatter her a little; how she laps it up. Oh Sasha. Can you believe she's started wearing eyeliner and shortie tops? It's very hard for a mother to see her lumpen daughter putting on a show of such shallow sexuality. I've always told her, "Darling you are LUCKY you're not a man magnet."

Because it does make life very difficult. I mean, a case very much in point. Mike. The Rotter. On his very first night staying here, what happens? I'm in my black satin dressing gown, innocently coming back from the kitchen with my second glass of Evian past the door to Sasha's room, when the Rotter emerges. Fully clothed but not completely zipped and buttoned. And what does he do when he sees me? "Goodnight then, Janey," he says, and looms close to peck me on the cheek, I can smell his breath and feel his crisp shirt against me and somehow I turn my head at the wrong moment, and well, it's almost tongues. When we are disengaged, he whispers, "That's right." And then he puts his hands on me, just lightly. "That's right," says Mike again, and goes back into Sasha's room.

They've gone out, I suppose. Although they can't have gone very far without the car battery. Gerald rang earlier. I said, "Gerald who?" as if the name meant nothing, but I knew perfectly well who it was, I just wanted to give him a hard time. I'd asked him to my birthday dinner on Friday, and he was ringing for details. He said that at Woodlands, he had noticed I had a very positive pink AURORA. I said I don't know about that, but I am a spring person, and actually talking of pink I'm still all soft from the seaweed wrap as it happens, hurry, hurry, roll up, Gerald, anybody, it'll wear off by the weekend – although of course I didn't say that. I just said it's nice to talk to someone who appreciates your aurora. I never know with the Rotter whether he's looking at me or not. He stroked the back of my neck the next time he stayed. Sasha had gone up to bed but although I was tired I – well, I don't know, but I particularly wanted to see the football. And we were sitting there alone watching England play Spurs I think, and he reached out and touched me, just lightly. I had on a rather good push-up bra under a beautiful cream angora sweater, so it was nice to know it worked, and besides this is my house, you know, I can do what I like.

Sometimes I think I imagined it. The thing on the landing. The angora moment. When I look at him when

Sasha's around, or even when she isn't sometimes, it's like looking into a mirror that doesn't reflect.

Scene Three: background sound of beauty parlour. Celtic mood music. She is very relaxed

Sasha's present to me was a facial (to be honest, I did hint), so I'm having it now before the birthday dinner tomorrow night. With Megan, who is an absolute dear and massages my hands at the same time and tells me all the gossip about the other girls during the part when I can't speak without cracking the mask and ruining it.

[*Serious*] There's a moment when they stroke your face, the Megans and the Maureens – and suddenly they go down to your neck, and sort-of gather you in, smoothing your neck and shoulders, even your ears. Sort of scooping you and caressing, scooping and caressing – and do you know, it makes me want to cry. Isn't that silly? [*She is upset*] I don't tell people, but once I did dabble in colonic irrigation, and it was frightfully weird and I certainly wouldn't do it again now I know it involves your bottom, but the woman stroked my tummy so tenderly as she operated the extractor pump, or whatever it was, that I really did burst into tears. Blubbed. In Beauchamp Place. The woman said it happened all the time. She seemed awfully nice at first. She said we're taught to think all our feelings are deep, deep inside, but actually, for most people, they are right on the surface. After all, the skin is our biggest organ, she said. "Would it be the size of a football pitch if you rolled it out?" I said; "I think I read that somewhere." And she stopped rubbing my tummy and said of course your skin's not the size of football pitch, how could it possibly be? And I said, Oh, I'm sorry, I'm always getting things wrong. But I thought there was no need for her to ruin the mood like that. I was only trying to join in.

Scene Four: evening of the birthday; she's a bit drunk; sipping wine as she talks; music in background

Sometimes I wonder how much I love Sasha. She won't let me say anything to her. And of course, all her life, she hasn't let me touch her. [*Drinks*] As a baby she screamed pretty well constantly, so it was hard to tell whether she was particularly distressed when I held her and nursed her. But later, there was no room for doubt, really. If I tried to pick her up, she would hit my face, or kick and scream. Doctor Hughes said it wasn't personal. I wasn't to take it personally. If Sasha has a touch taboo, it's her problem, not yours. She doesn't want your physical affection, Mrs Phipps, he said; and there's no point feeling aggrieved. "It's a one-way street, being a parent," he said. That's where I first heard the expression, I think: the one-way street. And I thought, well, I wouldn't mind a one-way street if things moved along it. But unfortunately ours seems to be a one-way street that's been gridlocked for the past twenty-one years.

I used to watch mothers blowing raspberries on their babies' stomachs, cuddling them, clasping them. I still do. Mothers petting their babies; holding hands to cross the road; primping the hair on their grown-up daughters. It's such a natural thing – to reach out. [*She starts to cry*] She lets the Rotter touch her. She lets him touch her in front of me.

Gerald rang. [*Drinks*] I was just getting ready for tonight, and thinking no, lemon socks, sorry, I really can't lower my standards, and he rang up to say he couldn't make it after all, he had a lecture on "Give and take in modern relationships", but happy birthday Mrs P and perhaps he'd see me next time I was at Woodlands. I was furious. The facial. The seaweed. The incredibly clean navel. Do people think I do all this for my own benefit? I told him he was hardly in a position to lecture other people on give and take when he was clearly incapable of commitment himself, and I pitied anybody who had a modern relationship with him, I was certainly well off out of it myself, perhaps he was the one who needed professional help! He said quietly, "This is ridiculous, I hardly know you, Janey," and I shouted, "That's not the point. That's not the point. I'm thinking if this is how you treat me, how must you treat other people? I've a good mind to report you to Woodlands." And he said, "I think I detect a few rejection issues, Janey!" And he hung up.

[*Drinks*] I do wish them well, you know, Sasha and Mike. They said they'd be back from the office at 7.30, the table is booked for nine. I'll tell them Gerald was too much in awe of me; too afraid of what might happen. They'll understand. Sasha has never been very keen on my boyfriends, anyway. So she'll be happy. Or perhaps I'll say I told him not to come? For her sake, I mean. That's it. I didn't want a stranger here. Because it's true. More than anything, I want my daughter to be happy. [*Listens*] They're home. [*Deep breath, puts down drink*] It's not my fault if Mike fancies me. The point is, whatever happens, she must never know.

Scene Five: steam bath/sauna; she's agitated; it's hot

They said I can have a few minutes in the sauna before I see Maureen. It's so hot in here! I mean, I know that's the point. But there's a limit, surely. It's dark too. And they sent me the high-fibre muesli when they know I prefer the fruit. They'll say, well, that's what happens when you turn up at a health farm in the middle of the night. And I'll say, yes, but it costs a fortune to come here to Woodlands, and you ought to make sure the night receptionist is properly trained, and besides you trade on people having a bad self-image, that's what Sasha says, you trade on people having a bad self-image, so if my self-image is really really bad at the moment, if I turn to you because I need you, I shouldn't have to face an inquisition to get in! But that's what it felt like, like arguing your way into Soviet China or something. "No luggage?" he said. He seemed quite suspicious, just because I didn't have any luggage, and was still in my cerise birthday taffeta. But in the end, he gave me a key to a top-of-the-range chalet; said they'd try to fit me into this morning's massage schedule. "This isn't a hotel," he explained, more than once. "I know!" I said. "I'm a regular patron! For heaven's sake, I only went home on Wednesday!" "I just wondered if you thought this was a hotel. Some people do. There's a Travelodge up the road." "I want to stay here!" I said. "I want to see Maureen! I know precisely what I want. Thank you!"

So why doesn't it feel right? It doesn't feel right at all. Perhaps when I've seen Maureen; when she's stroked it all away ...? Or Gerald! I could talk to Gerald, I'm sure of it. I mean, obviously we've had our ups and downs lately, but if I'm big enough to put them behind me, I'm sure he ought to be too. Life without drama wouldn't be very interesting, would it, that's what I'll say to him. It's what I used to say to Sasha, of course.

So they turned up at 7.30, and I was ready. The backless taffeta was something I'd been saving for ages, and when she came in Sasha was so nice about the effort I'd made that I was truly quite touched. "Happy birthday, Mum, you look foxy," she said, spotting me in the sitting room and leading Mike in with her. "Great shoes," added Mike. I was touched, but the moment I started to show it, "Oh don't cry, Mum," Sasha said. "Don't start." So I sniffed a bit and dabbed my eyes very carefully. But it was lovely to hear her say something nice. "You look lovely too, Sasha," I said. And yes, all right, it wasn't exactly true, but there was no need for her to get so impatient straight away. "Like, RIGHT," she said. "I look 'lovely'." "But you do," I said. She took a deep breath and started to leave the room. "Mike," I said. "Tell her she's lovely." "I'm going to the off licence," said Sasha. And although she walked quietly out of the house, I noticed she slammed the door.

Which left me alone with Mike. "Sasha hates attention, I don't know why," I said. "She's a lovely girl. She's always hated having her photograph taken; I'm surprised she's going out with a photographer." Mike made a square frame in the air using right-angled fingers and thumbs, looked at me through it with one eye closed. I smiled at him. Struck a pose. He rolled off the sofa, and pretended to take urgent pictures from the floor, on his knees, while I did the fashion model thing of turning, smiling, frowning, simpering, pointing my chin at different corners of the room. It felt quite natural. "You're very game, Janey," he said. I took it as a compliment. Of course it was an odd moment to remind me he was a photographer, but on the other hand, I was beginning to think he was an odd chap altogether. Sasha is no catch, as I may have said already. Even as her own mother, I have to admit Mike's the first person who's shown the slightest interest in her. "I wonder if I should go after her," I said, getting up. But I didn't get far. He pushed me back down, sat beside me. "I need to say something, Janey," said Mike. "I know," I said, softly. I knew what he was going to say. He was going to say that it was madness, but he couldn't resist me. He took my hand. I held my breath. "Janey?" "Yes, Mike." "I want to say this in the nicest possible way, Janey. But basically, could you stop coming on to me, please, because it's really, really embarrassing."

[*Pretending to make light of it*] Crikey, it's hot in here. They should do something about the thermostat, it can't be good for you. Hard to breathe. Anyway, we were side by side on the couch, Mike and I, and the lights were low – that's just the way it was, I hadn't arranged it. And I suddenly felt this awful desperation. Mike might say he didn't want me, but I knew he did. I get things wrong a lot, I know I do, it's true, but I don't get that thing wrong. I've never, ever got that thing wrong. So I leaned across, put my hands to his face, and kissed him. And for a few seconds I had him, he put his arms round me, held me tightly, oh so close, and kissed me back. And then, then he quite roughly pushed me away. At which point Sasha walked back in with a bottle of champagne. And I felt something heavy drop out of my body and roll away.

Patsy, the cool lady who runs the steam room, just told me Maureen isn't on duty today. She peered through the heavy-aired gloom to see who was using the sauna, and did a double-take – surprised to see me back so soon, you see. "Did you not go home just a couple of days ago, Mrs Phipps?" she said. I laughed yes, yes, couldn't keep away. Patsy frowned. She came in and shut the door. "You don't want to get addicted to treatments, Mrs Phipps." Don't worry, I won't do that, I said. It was hard to concentrate on the here and now, I had been thinking of all those times on holiday when I rubbed sun cream into Sasha's infant back and she screamed and struggled and ran away half done. "I'm only doing this because I love you," I used to say, as I held her wrists. "I love you, Sasha. Why do you have to fight me?"

Patsy was still going on, though. "I'm serious," she was saying. "There's a limit to the benefits –" and then she stopped. She could see I was on the verge of crying, I suppose. So she sighed and sat next to me on the bench, even though she was fully clothed, and the place was burning hot. "What are we going to do with you?" she said, sitting down. I looked down at my slim arms, my smooth legs, the beautiful manicure, the all-over skin of a thirty-year-old. "You look lovely already, Mrs Phipps," she said. "I'm a spring person," I said. And Patsy the steam-room lady put her arm around me, and squeezed me very tight.

The Father

JOHN is nice, and quite funny; a bit slow and often charmingly self-amused, as if he's done a lot of drugs. While he talks about being dynamic, he isn't. His big problem is that he's always trying to suppress unpleasant feelings and worries, but isn't very successful at it. Because of what's recently happened to him, he is very vulnerable.

Scene One: cello practice in background; low-ish level with occasional scrapings; very persistent, however. A simple, sad piece. Whoever is playing this – it's actually John's twelve-year-old son David, heard from another room – is determined to learn. John is attempting to sort some vinyl records; he is having a fag, and very relaxed

[*Inhales*] The thing about these old records, [*he flips a couple of albums*] is that half of 'em I don't even recognise. Which is a bit disturbing, if you know what I mean. [*Flip*] I mean, I'm not gonna let it bother me, but in among me Sex Pistols and me Paul Weller and what have you, I seem to of got, look, Rostropovich doing the Elgar, [*looks at it, a bit confused*] and I'm not being funny, but when you fancy a nice old head-bang at midnight, like, which is when you normally start rummaging through this sort of old stuff, it's not Rostropovich doing the Elgar that you automatically reach for. [*Looks at it again*] Must be Kaff's. I'm not gonna let it worry me, though. No, no, not worth worrying about. "Some fings are worth worrying about, John, and some fings aren't. Your trouble is you've got too much imagination." It's a mystery, that's all. [*Smokes*] Perhaps a burglar broke in and left 'em, eh? Ha. Coz there's loads more, look. [*Flips*] Jacqueline Du Pré. [*Flip, flip, flip*] Pablo Casals. Paul Tortelier. Well, at least I'm starting to spot a theme, eh? Kaff must of forgotten to tell me about them, that's all. The thing is, they can't be David's, can they, coz, well, he's twelve. And twelve-year-olds, even when they're [*proud of him*] top-of-the-class prodigies on the old vi-o-lon-cello like David is, they don't go in for scratchy Deutsche Grammophon at thirty-three and a third. It's all digital with kids. Oh yeah. Twenty thousand tracks on a device the size of a stick of chewing gum, that's the way of it now. Mrs Watson, she's David's cello teacher, she was telling me about it, kids downloading the equivalent of all the music in this room – hours and bloody hours of it – onto these tiny white machines. Amazing, really. A lot of the kids at work have got 'em. You'd think, at a call centre, you'd get enough of headphones, wouldn't you? I know I do. I got ears like hotplates by the end of the day. You could put me on me side, like, and use me as a hostess trolley. [*Inhales thoughtfully*] Yeah, stick of chewing gum! Or packet of chewing gum. Or packet of fags anyway. [*Thinks about it*] Either way, ha, I can't think of anything worse.

I love Saturday mornings. No call centre. No bus. No bleeding grief counsellor! David doing his practice – [*Up on David's cello, then John gently shuts the door on it*] That's lovely, that is. I'm dead proud of him, you know. He's only been playing a year! A lot of kids would of piled on the agony at a time like this, you know, but not David. Kaff always said, he's so SANE, David is, it's a miracle, babe, when you look at the pair of us! Ha. So while David gets on with becoming the next Pablo Casals, like, Saturday's my chance to clear my head a bit, attack some sorting, change the beds, do the washing, have a sit-down, flip through Kaff's old Delias. [*He turns some pages in a recipe book*] Kaff used to love this book. Beats me why. Look at this one. "Wild Mushrooms in Madeira En Croûte with Foaming Hollandaise. This recipe is ideal for entertaining: make the filling and pastry parcels THE DAY BEFORE." [*Can't cope with this idea*] Now, I'm not being funny, but that does my head in. I mean, how can you start making your pastry parcels THE DAY BEFORE, when it's already the day AFTER the day before? Makes no sense, does it? And I read a bit of Kierkegaard in my time, yeah, I'm not stupid. [*Lights fag*] I might add this is not the sort of behaviour you would of expected from Delia, either – spreading existential doubt on a nice Saturday morning. [*Inhales*] No, but I feel proper dynamic on Saturdays. Beds, washing, recipes, advanced philosophical problems, you name it. Oh yeah.

[*Pause; he doesn't move; inhales smoke sharply*] The thing is, I can't tell anybody, but the idea of all those records sort of miniaturised and packed into a stick of chewing gum, I find that quite disturbing, to be honest. I'm not being funny. I know you don't really get all those tiny classical musicians all sort of squashed in – like "Honey I Shrunk the Berlin Philharmonic conducted by Sir Simon Rattle." But it's kind of a worrying idea, that's what I'm saying. [*Smokes*] All those cellists in microscopic morning suits, sort of jostling and fighting for elbow room – like, you know, musical spermatozoa. Violinists all cheek-by-jowl and poking each others' eyes out with their pointy bows. You can imagine 'em, can't you, all screaming and screaming and suffocating and climbing on top of each other and banging on the walls. Ha. [*Smokes and thinks*] Don't bear thinking about, does it?

(*Tries to gather himself*) Right. Lunch, think about lunch or something – although not wild mushrooms in madeira en croûte with foaming sauce, because apart from not having any wild mushrooms, or madeira, or foam, or in fact anything in the fridge except a tub of Flora, I would of needed to start it yesterday as it turns out, as if I was a psychic or something. [*Can't let this go*] I mean, perhaps they should start a new branch of cooking, like, I'm not being funny. The Clairvoyant Kitchen. Psychic Cuisine. Mystic Mince. That could really catch on, that could. You'd get all the ingredients listed, like: eight ounces of flour, cup of sugar, you know, pinch of salt, the usual, and then "Eggs – well, you just GUESS how many eggs, Madame Arcarti, if you know everything else already."

[*Pause; he stubs out the fag*] I'm wondering if David's bed'll go another week. I'll ask him, he's a good kid. [*Door opens; the practising can be heard again*] No, I won't disturb him. [*As he shuts the door, whispers proudly*] You'd never guess what he's been through, would you?

[*Not enthusiastic*] So. Beans on toast it is, then. David

won't mind. He can handle anything. "Dad," David always says, "don't worry. Beans on toast is great." And then he does the toast, and puts the kettle on. [*Pause*] And then he does the beans as well, come to think of it. You know I'm dead impressed by how he's taken to that cello; he used to be such an outdoor kid, Kaff and I hardly ever saw him. But I suppose everything changed, didn't it?

You know what? I'll put the kettle on. Get things started. [*An "Uff!" of effort as he leans across to press the kettle switch; it comes to the boil during next bit*] The funny thing is, see, I wanted to play the cello when I was his age! I can't remember what happened to stop me, except – [*remembers*] well, of course, I asked my dad outright, didn't I – [*it's hilarious that he was so stupid*] I asked me dad! – and ha, that put the kibosh right on it. Ha. I never learned! He was such a nasty bloke, my dad, God rest him! (*Laughs*) Kaff couldn't stand him! She was dead angry on my behalf, like, when I told her about him not letting me have a cello. "That was cruel, John! That was so cruel!" The thing is, he was that perverse with us kids when we was small. Sally, she knew how to deal with him, she was clever, and she used to say, John, listen, it's ever so, ever so easy. You have to pretend you DON'T want something, and then you stand a chance of getting it. See? But if you make a fuss, if you let on it's important to you, Dad'll just love not letting you have it! Funny now to remember being a kid. Don't seem real, all that terror. Like it happened to someone else, in the nineteenth century or something, in a cruel northern orphanage. Once, when little Pete was desperate for a pet, see, Dad found out, so he gave ME a big rabbit, coz he knew I didn't care one way or the other. That's how it worked. [*Remembers*] Ginger! Yeah, Dad gave me Ginger and said I mustn't share him with little Pete under any circumstances, but I did, and when Dad found out, he was furious and put Ginger in a suitcase and sold him to some geezer up the pub. We were six and four at the time. Pete went mental. But I think Dad done his best, you know, for all that; he just didn't know what to do with children, except sort of niggle them.

[*Kettle has boiled; John spoons instant coffee into cup, adds water etc.*] And now David's taken to the cello, twelve years old, see, so it's all come right, see. He's a terrific kid, the way he's handled everything. He's been a rock over the past year; an inspiration. And the way he practises all the time – it's like the opposite of what everyone says: kids moaning on about being made to stay indoors and do their scales and that. I have to tear the thing out of his hands sometimes. Mrs Watson says she's never seen progress like it! And it's all self-motivated, that's the thing, no pressure from me; I hate that, I used to see it when Kaff's brother was coaching them under-elevens, it was terrible the way them dads pushed the little boys. No, this was all David's idea. It's two days after the funeral, I remember, and I've just jacked in my manager's job coz of not coping, and I've been locking myself away a bit, like, so as not to frighten the boy, and David says, "Dad, I want to play the cello, can you afford it?", and I'm proper chuffed and say, well, afford it or not, I'll arrange the lessons, and he says I've already done that, Dad, and all you got to do is pay Mrs Watson in Thames Street, and I say what about an instrument, and he says I got a second-hand one picked out, Dad, so you don't have to worry about that neither. And since then he's been at it night and day.

[*Dismay*] Is that the time? Blimey, right, beans en croûte with can't-believe-it's-not-foaming-hollandaise. [*Pause*] Assuming we got some bread.

Scene Two: the sound of cello practice; he's not as comfortable as before

All right, how does this thing work? [*Fiddles with something mechanical – it's a quite old-fashioned tape recorder*] Allo, allo, allo, testing, testing, one-two, one-two. [*Rewind and play: "testing, one-two, one-two". He stops the machine, and takes a deep breath*] I'm not sure about this, at all. But all right. They said, "John, you can always wipe it if there's something you don't want us to hear." So I say, I'm not being funny, mate, but if I wipe everything I don't want YOU to hear, it'll be a bloody blank tape. They mean well, I know that. It's just that they can't half get on me nerves as well. [*Imitates posh person*] "It might help DAVID if you do this," they said. "Have you talked to David? Have you cried yet? If you cry, John, perhaps you can both move forward." I mean, what's all that about? I said, [*surprised*] "David's all right, thanks, he's got a cello." And they look at each other, see, like I'm soft in the head, and I think, well, THAT'S why I don't say very much, there's no mystery.

Better shut the door. [*Door shuts; cello muffled*] Now. [*Rustle of paper as he sits down and consults his instructions*] I made some notes. [*Wry laugh*] Ha! Not very helpful. "Talk about Kaff." [*Turns paper over*] That's it. Well, look, oh get on with it, John, get on with it.

[*Recorder is turned on. From now on, John is recording himself and a bit self-conscious, but is concentrating more than he usually does, rambling less, taking himself a bit more seriously*]

All right. [*Clears throat*] I'm NOT gonna talk about Kaff, actually, I'm going to talk about something else – because, let's face it, you're not here and you can't make me. Ha. And besides, I'm not being funny, but I can't help noticing that whatever I talk about, you always say, "Ooh, that's all part of the grieving process, John," so it occurs to me I could say anything and you'd never act surprised. Say I said, "I've developed this taste for salad cream sandwiches with hay in them," you'd say, "Ah. Hay sandwiches! A recognised stage in the grieving process. Tell us how you feel about hay in general." Honest, I could really have you on if I felt like it. "I dreamed about being a Shetland pony on a windy beach," I could say. "I could feel the breeze lift the mane from my neck, and hear the seagulls calling, 'Kaff! Kaff'." I mean, that's just my imagination, see? That's my trouble, Kaff always said: too much imagination. She didn't tell me all sorts of things, you know, because she didn't want me to worry or get obsessed, like. "I know what you're like," she'd say. "You're a Mister Worry Guts, you can't let things go." And I know she meant well, but that would really do my head in. We argued about it all the time. She'd say, "John, it's because I love you that I don't tell you things." But I'd say, "If you don't tell me things, Kaff, you don't love me!" We never got it sorted, not even at the end. Blimey, I was the last to hear about that tumour being inoperable; her bloody second cousin's husband knew about it before I did. But anyway, sorry, my point is: say I told you that this pony and seagull dream was true, you'd be going, "Oh that's good, John, that's very good. The seagull dream! How did you feel as the pony? Are you ready to cry yet? You see, this is all part of the grieving process!"

Anyway, what I want to talk about, after all that, is my dad. Ha. That surprised you! I was thinking about him the other day, see, and kind of fondly remembering the old bastard, and now I can't stop thinking about him, and the more I think about him, see, the more upset I get. Well, you did ask. [*He is talking calmly*] I feel ... furious. I've never felt this angry in my life, all right? And if you can believe it, it's over a cello! [*Warming*] I mean, this was nearly thirty years ago. I hadn't thought about it for years till the other day. And I don't even know where I got the idea in those days, it was crackers, kids like me didn't play musical instruments, and how could he afford it, it was daft. So I keep trying to think of something else, obviously – But if I try and think of something else, see, this fury just wells up and, and, and I want to kill him. IS THIS ALL PART OF THE GRIEVING PROCESS? Coz if it is, you can keep it.

[*Big effort; pulls himself together*] It's not the cello, as such. Course it isn't. I got over that. I just keep thinking, fancy bringing up a kid, training him, like, never to say what he wants, or tell you what's upset him – always to cover himself up with some sort of camouflage, coz otherwise his own dad will grab the information and use it to hurt him. I mean, I don't want to blow my own trumpet, but [*pride*] look at David. Look at the contrast. All right, his mum died. And all right, everyone's on at me – his teachers, the grief people, even Mrs bloody Watson – everyone's saying this constant cello thing is a bit, you know, funny. They keep asking if Kaff loved that sort of music, and I say, [*defensive*] "What if she did? There's nothing morbid about this." He's a lucky kid; that's what they ought to see; I mean, he's lucky for a start, isn't he, that I'm not the sort of bloke to break into his room, grab his cello from him and sell it down the Princess Alice! Blimey, I'm even a bit jealous of him sometimes, you know. Jealous of my own kid. Coz, let's face it: when HE says, out of the blue, "Dad, I'd like a cello," I get him a cello! [*Anger*] And there's nothing FUNNY about David practising. He's getting on. He's handling it. He's coping. If David WASN'T coping – [*surprising vehemence*] well, just don't tell me that; don't anyone ever tell me that; oh stop it, this is stupid! [*Grabs machine*] How do you stop this thing? [*Fumbles with buttons*] How do you stop it! [*He recovers; deep breath*] All right.

[*Opens door; cello practice comes in; big sigh of reassurance*] That's better. [*Emotional, but not crying*] I'm so proud of that boy. I love him so much, you know. I'd bloody die for him. And he loved Kaff so much, oh it would of broke your heart.

Scene Three: the cello is playing faintly; it's quite early in the morning and John is in bed, just woken up by the sound

What? What, oh no. [*Coughs; switches on light*] Oh gawd, twenty to seven. [*For the first time, he is uncomfortable about the cello; it's making him feel guilty, so he sounds irritable*] I wish he'd knock that off. I know it's important to the kid, I know that. But, you know, blimey. A laugh's a laugh.

[*A big sigh; he sits up and arranges himself against pillows etc.; coughs, lights up fag*] We had a day out yesterday, David and me. It was what you might call an unmitigated disaster. The thing was, Mrs Watson give me a hard time again when I picked David up Tuesday night; she said I ought to spend more quality time with him, see, away from the music. She said it would be an improvement, in fact, if we spent any time together at all. It might help us to "move on". Everyone's an expert on me and David, see; everyone's our unofficial counsellor; that's what happens when you're bereaved. [*Smokes*] It's not an uninteresting process, I'll say that. Suddenly, instead of being a viable human being with a job and a family, see, who can be trusted to get on with his own life, you're just this sort of big emotional blobby thing that people feel they can all take a poke at with a sharp stick. It's like you got a sign on you: "Come on, give us a poke; if you draw blood, you get a prize." Like that woman visiting the old lady in the hospice, when Kaff was dying, complete stranger, she took me aside and said, [*loud whisper*] "You and David will have to be brave for each other now." And you got to take it, that's the funny thing. When there's death going on, you got to say, all grateful, with tears in your eyes, "Do you know, Mrs Doodah, that's so wise you ought to write it down," when what you really want to do is punch her in the face, or at least point out that her son is wearing a T-shirt with "Megadeth" printed on it, which is far from tactful in a hospice. She said the same to David, as well, this woman. I heard her. [*Whisper*] "You'll have to brave for each other, you and your dad." Brave for each other? Of course we're brave for each other, silly cow. We know that much, thank you, we're not stupid.

Took me a little while to come up with a scheme for a day out, though, coz I didn't want David to smell a rat, like. I mean, if I said, all casual, "Son, how about a bit of a knockabout down the park?" he'd of thought, now, that's a bit odd, Dad bloody hates football and so do I. And there was lots of things I couldn't suggest coz they'd of reminded him of his mum. Then I remembered how he'd always fancied a go on that London Eye, you know, and I thought, well, I COULD handle that, it's only half an hour, I don't have to spend the whole time on it picturing, you know, a fatal catastrophe. There's no need to dwell on the way it might break off its spindle, like, and then with this terrible roaring, trumpeting noise like a dying elephant, roll along the river-bed of the Thames and crash into Waterloo Bridge all buckled like a wrecked bicycle wheel. And meanwhile all the people in the glass bubbles getting thrown about like grains of sand in an egg-timer and suffocating and dying under water and ending up as the first item on the *Six O'Clock News*.

The thing about David is that he looks ever so much like his mum, have I said that? Light-blue eyes, all alive and watchful. And when he laughs – oh blimey, when he laughs he's the spitting image. And he's dead quick like she was. "You're not going to worry about this, Dad?" he said as we stepped into the gondola thing. [*Brave laugh*] "Course not," I said. "Course not. Come on, David, this'll be lovely." Then the door closed on the little group we were destined to share our lovely watery grave with, and we started to rise up in the air, swinging a bit, and I shut my eyes and thought about how, if I sorted out the room with the records in it, we could set up that old ping-pong table Kaff's mum give us; and then I thought how strange it was that David don't play computer games like other kids and is it my fault, I bet it's my fault for not encouraging him or asking other kids round to play, but when does encouragement become interference, and when does interference become bullying, and would I be a better dad if I sat him down and said, "TALK to me about your mum, David," but on the other hand what kid wants a ping-pong table these days, you must be crackers, John, and when I opened my eyes we'd only travelled about a foot into the air and I thought, mm, this is going to be a test, then.

Obviously I was disappointed. I'd had this romantic idea, see, that when we was way up in the blue sky and the fluffy clouds, like, perhaps me and David would finally just speak to each other about Kaff and everything. I'd forgotten it might be overcast and raining – which it was – and that there'd be other damp and steaming people in our capsule, in any case, some of them foreigners, jabbering away and misidentifying London landmarks through the murk, and that in any case I'd be mostly listening for the fatal snap of a cable, and trying to work out whether the drop would kill us first (before we drowned). And it never occurred to me, either, that David might be frightened. But he was, you know. I'm pretty sure he was. He went all white and sweaty and he wouldn't look at me. I didn't know what to do – it was so unlike him, he's been so strong.

"This is good, isn't it, David?" I say, all nonchalant. "See that thing over there that those people just said was the Cenotaph? That's Cleopatra's Needle, point of fact." He nods but doesn't say anything, and keeps looking in the other direction. "Look, there's Thames Street, where Mrs Watson lives," I say. "Mm," he says, with his eyes closed. He just won't look at me; it's horrible. So I try another tack, try talking about home instead, to take his mind off it. "David," I say, "I found some old records in the living-room, do you think they could have been your mum's, it's just she never mentioned them." And he looks up at me, almost fierce, and says, [*he's still upset by what David said*] "Look, stop it, Dad." Just like that. "Stop it, Dad." Well, I'm hurt. I say, "What? Stop what?" And he says, "Stop worrying! Look, if people don't tell you things, it's only because they love you!" And I think, "Whoa!" I think, "Oh my God, David." And I look out at the big rainy sky above the big rainy town and I think, well, that's that for me and David, then. We've had it.

[*Cello*]

[*Dead*] I wish he'd stop. I do really.

Scene Four: the cello is playing something mournful throughout the scene; as the scene progresses, we realise this is a good thing, but at first it is ambiguous. John is having another look at the records; he's hurt

[*He flips*] So these ARE Kaff's records, then. I asked her sister and she told me. [*Flip*] Apparently, she loved them, but she used to hide them from me, you know, the usual thing: protect John by lying to him; protect John by excluding him; don't tell him anything and then say it was love and concern what stopped you. I mean, if she was here, I'd have a right go at her. You know what she thought? Well, I reckon she thought if I heard these records, I'd get upset remembering my horrible old dad, and how he was so "cruel" to me when I wanted a cello. So she shared them with David instead, and the upshot is – and this is dead funny, this is – the upshot is he now plays "Air on a Bloody G String" all day and all night, so it didn't work, Kaff, did it? It didn't work in any case! That's what you call irony, that is. Oh what a mess. Blimey, I'd of been able to cope with a bit of Paul Tortelier once in a while, Kaff. I'm just a bit of a worrier; I'm not a bloody psycho.

It wasn't easy, but I went and asked Mrs Watson what the hell was going on, like. I was sick of it. There's this boy in the house, see, this lovely boy, and I've been loyally defending him against everyone, saying he's doing brilliantly, coping brilliantly, handling it, but it turns out, I'm not being funny, I've only been doing that because I'm stupid. So I say, all right, Mrs Watson, you tell me. Here's the theories so far. I produce this list. [*Rustle of paper*] They may entertain you in their diversity, if nothing else, I say. [*Ahem*] All right, David plays all the time because [*reads*]:

One. He's a nutter, like his dad – no, listen, I'm not being funny.

Two. He's communing in some morbid way with his dead mum.

Three. [*He likes this one*] He's successfully taking his mind off his dead mum by concentrating on practical matters such as bow technique.

Four. [*He hates this one*] He's being brave for his dad's sake.

And five – oh yeah, I threw this one in, for good measure – he just happens to really like the cello.

[*Paper folded up*] Well, she's dead angry, as it happens. She doesn't like my list at all. She implies it's none of the above, like, and things get a bit heated. "Do you actually listen to him playing?" she keeps saying. "Listen?" I say. [*Scoffing*] "Of course I listen. Not much option in a house that size. I'm just glad he didn't choose the alpine horn, mate, that's the only thing that could of made it worse." "He wants you to hear him, John, THAT'S WHY HE PLAYS," she says. And I say, [*exasperated*] "Look, I hear him all the time!" "No you don't!" she says. "All right, John, what do you FEEL when you hear him playing?" "Oh, don't you start!" I say, and I walk out.

[*Cello*]

And I come back here. I mean, what does she mean, LISTEN? I'm always listening to him. I wish he'd talk to me, that's all, instead of sawing away at that big hollow box from dawn till dusk. They ask every time down at Grief HQ, "Have you talked to David yet? Have you cried yet? If you cry, John, perhaps you can both move forward." And I say, [*he knows he's been wrong about this now, though*] "For the last time, David's all right, he don't need to talk to me, if he did, he would."

[*Cello*]

I'm worn out with it. It wears you out, loving people and losing them, and trying to judge what's best for the survivors. I mean, I'm just a bloke, how am I supposed to know how to comfort a kid who's lost his mum? He didn't sleep, you know, all the time she was in that hospice. He didn't eat. He clung to her at the end; poor Kaff, it must of been heart-breaking to see him like that, [*it's getting to him*] like his whole little life was being snuffed out.

[*The cello swells*]

I'm doing my best, Kaff. I been trying so hard not to push him. And all this time – I'm so stupid. [*Overwhelmed, starts to weep*] All this time he's been telling me how he feels, hasn't he? In the music. He's been telling me how he feels and I wasn't even listening!

[*He opens the door and calls, in distress*] David!

[*The cello stops*]

[*Softly*] Oh, David, David, I'm so sorry.

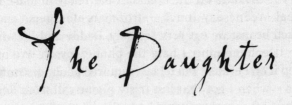

The Daughter

JUDY is clever, sharp, deeply defensive.

Scene One: afternoon TV in background

Dad keeps asking, "So who was it? Who was it, Judykins? Have you got a secret admirer?" So thank you, God, as Basil Fawlty used to say. Thank you so much. I had just got back from my daily excursion to Mac Fisheries. I mean, I'm well aware it's a Tesco Metro; I do know that. It's just Daddy likes the old names – or perhaps he thinks I like the old names – anyway, it's nobody's business if we prefer to talk about James Walker's and Lilly and Skinner's. "Popping in to Timothy White's for some more of your fly-away hair shampoo?" Daddy says. "You've got a boyfriend in there you're not telling me about." It's nice to remember Timothy White's. I don't care what anyone else thinks. We don't lead our lives for other people.

So, I'd just got back from Mac Fisheries, you see, and I'd put the bags on the breakfast bar ready to make the usual Wednesday lunch – frozen beefburgers, mash, baked beans; we eat very sensibly, Daddy and I – when the telephone rang. I hate the phone, myself. We only keep it on because when I last inquired about disconnection – when I got that last nasty phone call from Roger – the GPO said they would be "obliged" to take away our smart Trimphone and couldn't guarantee we'd get the same model again if we ever wanted to reconnect. "You won't get one of these again, sweetheart, these went out with the ark," the man joked, so I told him as far as I was concerned he could go out with the ark himself, and we'd keep the phone. Daddy wanted to keep it, I remember – not that he has anyone to call. We did his eightieth last month, and it was just us two. But he declared he'd pay the bill himself, and has done ever since. It comes in his name; I don't even see it. It's amazing the stubbornness of the old.

And now it was ringing. Trilling. You might say warbling. We both looked at it, and looked at each other, but in the end I answered. "Hello, this is St Margaret's 2622." "Judith!" said the person at the other end. I knew I shouldn't have said yes. But I was so relieved it wasn't him that I didn't think. "Jude, it's me!" this familiar voice said. "It's Beverley! Remember? From Richmond High!"

I sat down. "It's me! Bev!" she said again. Daddy was signalling at me, and I didn't know what to do, so I put my head down and let my hair swing forward like a curtain right around me and the receiver – the way I used to let it fall round my rough book at school. It's quite comforting to be able to do that. Daddy says they based the character in *The Addams Family* on me – the one that's all hair and shuffles along like a walking haystack. Glad that I couldn't see Daddy, I said quietly, "I'm afraid I can't talk at the moment. Can I take your number?" "Oh," she said. "Sorry, is this a bad time? Call me. I'm at the paper till about 1.30 on – got a pen? I'm on 0-2-0-7, blah, blah, blah; blah, blah, blah." I don't know what she said, I didn't write it down, I just made uh-huh noises to make it sound as if I was. "Then my mobile is 0-7-7, blah, blah, and my home is 0-2-0-8, blah." She seemed very proud of all these numbers. "Are you on e-mail?" she said. "No." "Well, just in case, the address is Beverley, dot, Brayfield, dot, blah, dot, uk, dot, blah – at blah-blah."

The beefburgers weren't quite right. The same box; but they didn't taste the same. They think you'll put up with that kind of thing, but I shall speak to Mr Thomas tomorrow. He might give me a voucher for Carnation milk or something. Bev sounded like she might ring again if I didn't call her back, so when Daddy was having his afternoon nap with *Godspell* playing on the music centre (my choice; he prefers Radio Four), I quietly laid down the cryptic crossword we'd started, and unplugged the phone from the wall. I'd just worked out "Harassed nurse left with a sense of grievance" – something E, something E something T something something something – was "Resentful". An anagram of "Nurse" and "Left". Daddy and I enjoy our cryptics. Oddly enough, we can't do the quick, easy, five-minute sort at all.

I gave Daddy a little kiss on his bald head as I walked past, I can never resist it. [*Sings, reedily*] Day by day, to see thee more clearly, love thee more dearly. [*Stops singing*] Bloody Beverley Brayfield. Rings up after all this time and sets me off remembering Roger, and sets Daddy off on admirers. Daddy still harks on about the man from the

GPO, saying I only tried to get the telephone disconnected to get a man in the flat. And that was ten years ago. As for Mr Thomas's vouchers – I certainly won't mention them again to Daddy. "Vouchers, Judy? What's he giving you vouchers for? What have you been up to behind the sausage counter?"

Of course, when I knew Bev, when I did actually have admirers, Daddy used to guard my honour like a pitbull. I once had twelve people in my bedroom – four of them boys – sitting listening to a *Monty Python* record, and he made us all go outside because he imagined some sort of orgy would break out. It was just the way his mind worked. I didn't even tell him about Roger; I knew he would be wanting to know, "Have you done it yet?" and not believing me when I said I didn't want to.

Back in the sixth form, Bev was my best friend ever. Sixth-form mavericks, we were. Young hippy-style renegades in flared loons and badly stitched cheesecloth. We got Miss Watson to read out that notice in assembly: "The Non-Conformist Society will meet at midnight in the cupboard in Room Nine." That was us. Beverley and Judith. Bev and Jude. "Who was it on the phone, Judykins?" Daddy asked when he woke up. "Was it a secret ad –?" [*interrupts*] "It was Beverley Brayfield, Daddy," I yelled from the kitchen. "The one who neglects her mother and hates all men but you in particular." "Oh," he said. "Did those beefburgers seem all right to you?" I said. But when I came in, I found him holding the dead receiver to his ear, looking puzzled.

The Daughter

Scene Two: bathroom echoes, bath running

Since Mag died, I like to feel I've made things nice for Daddy. Mag didn't love him very much; just reminded him all the time what a big sacrifice she'd made bringing me up – when, after all, I was his "by-blow". Do people say "by-blow" now? Mag certainly did. In fact, she rarely constructed a sentence without it. Having taken in his by-blow (me) she just reproached him about it; reproached him till there was no breath left in her body; reproached him till she died. Now there was a harassed nurse with a sense of grievance. "What about MY life?" she used to say. And if I said, "What life's that then, Mag?" she'd bark, "Why do you always take HIS side?" No wonder Daddy worked such long hours running the sweet stall. He was a popular man; no one disliked Daddy except Mag. Mag was deranged. She accused him of seeing other women right up until the end. She said he saw prostitutes and everything. To listen to her, you'd think he had the sex drive of Frank Sinatra.

I went out to work at first myself, of course: got a nice job in Selfridges straight from school selling embroidery silks, fancy ribbons, rick-racks. They said I was a little over-qualified, with my A grades in French, Maths and English Literature, but I told them to disregard that. I was perfectly happy for rick-rack to be my life. I could call it rique-racque and apply calculus to the stock-take if they liked. They had no idea what I was talking about, but took me on. And I was very happy. But then, after about three years, they did the Great Haberdashery Consolidation and promoted me to executive luggage and I left, and I never went back to work again. I have to say they were surprised. Everyone was surprised. I was a bit surprised myself. But I just said it was only sensible to stay home. Mag was already ill; Daddy was sixty, but still worked from early in the morning till at least seven at night, long after the market closed at three. And of course there was the hair. Hair this long and fine takes three or four hours every morning to dry naturally. Ergo, you can't really go to work.

Scene Three

There's been knocking. It's bound to be her. I've had the phone unplugged for two days now – although oddly, when I got home from shopping at midday, the jack seemed to have moved closer to the plug than I remembered it. Daddy shouldn't be troubled with all this, I mean, he's eighty. I do try to protect him from what goes on out there. So when the knocking started I said to Dad, sit still, do nothing. Whoever it is will go away. So we watched *Watercolour Challenge* with the sound down and whispered together, "Hannah Gordon's holding up very well, isn't she? Do you think she's had a facelift?" – because you can't say NOTHING when *Watercolour Challenge* is on; it's just not humanly possible. In the end the knocking stopped, and the letterbox clanged. Beverley had put a note through, asking me to ring her. She adopted a very urgent tone; said she was worried about me. I think she should worry about herself; it's not normal behaviour, what she's doing. Hounding people in their own homes, when they just want to be left alone. Turning up to gloat about the life she's made for herself in the big wide world.

It was weird to think she was outside, right outside

the door. As I said, it's twenty years since the last time I saw her – on a day I have lots of reasons to remember. We had lunch to celebrate her rather mediocre English degree from York University and her new junior reporter job on a newspaper in Newcastle, meeting in Pizzaland in Oxford Street, where in those days they had alpine murals, pine benches, and waitresses got up like Heidi. It was one of those occasions when I was paying, but she condescended to me. We had a lot of those. Anyway, I remember Beverley said in a loud voice to expect inferior service from the Heidis "because we were both women" – a remark that made a deep impression, not just because she had to bring sex into everything, but because it was the first time I was ever referred to as a woman and I thought she was presumptuous to assume I wouldn't mind. After all, I don't much like it now, and back then I was only twenty-two.

We had a couple of glasses of the house red and we talked about her. I'd intended to tell her I'd met this nice chap called Roger in fancy hosiery, and that I'd been offered a promotion, but I didn't get a chance. It turned out she'd had an abortion in her third year and had done her entire degree on women writers, as a sort of protest against – well, against common sense, obviously – and they'd had to reorganise the course to accommodate her. "I am in the vanguard," she said. "Oh well, better than being in the guard's van," I quipped, rather amusingly. "I was quite famous for making a stand," she said. "There was a piece about me in the *Yorkshire Post*." Which, funnily enough, she happened to have with her, protected by a sheet of sticky-backed plastic. It was illustrated by a picture of her demonstrating outside an examination hall during the Shakespeare paper. "This examination discriminates against women," it said, on her placard – or almost. "There's only one 'm' in 'discriminate'," I said. Evidently she shouted things like "Scab!" and "Quisling!" at fellow female students going in, and was surprised when they had a party afterwards and didn't invite her.

I remember I said perhaps she should read some Shakespeare, she might enjoy it. Which I suppose was my mistake, because suddenly she was denouncing ME as a quisling and a scab. Out of the blue, I was a traitor in the gender war. "There's a picket line in your own home, Jude. And through emotional debility you side with the bosses against Mag!" Well, I laughed, but she wouldn't give it up. Emotional debility. Where did that come from? "Who are you reading at the moment?" she demanded. She seemed genuinely angry. As it happened, I was in the middle of an Agatha Christie binge, but I wasn't going to tell her that, so I said "Milton". "Ha!" she said. "Another man who tyrannised his females. Although at least he wasn't sex mad like your dad."

I pushed a bit of soggy pizza on to my fork, then put it down. "I'm going," I said. "Bev, I am not a quisling. And my dad is neither a tyrant nor a sex maniac. He's a warm and loving person." "Your dad exploits women, Jude," she called after me, as I got up and left. "You watch. He did it to Mag and he's done it to you. You're sexually retarded!" And I walked out of Pizzaland and went back to work in a turmoil. I felt hurt and angry, and I actually made an exceptionally good sale of a calfskin slimline briefcase that afternoon to an Arab gentleman for two hundred pounds, which was a bloody fortune in those days. It was that night I finally let Roger take me to the bedsit; and we drank some Newcastle Brown and I let him put my hand down his trousers. I remember he wanted me to open my eyes while the business was done but I gritted my teeth and tried to think about rick-rack. It was the day after that I decided to give up work to look after Daddy and never see Roger again, or ever go to Pizzaland for that matter.

Now Bev's on *Question Time* and *Newsnight* all the time. Writes a column in a newspaper giving equal weight to feminist outrage about equal pay and the three-figure haircuts a modern female columnist simply has to have if she spends half the year in Manhattan. She goes on fact-finding missions; turns up on *Woman's Hour* talking about her novels – so-called "postmodern" historical romances in which Charles the First says things like "As if", while Henrietta Maria goes salsa dancing. I don't know, I've never read them. I don't read anything published after 1960. But her mum stops me occasionally at her bus stop to boast about an American book tour or the latest invitation to Downing Street. I asked her how she tracked Bev's movements and she said, "Oh, I log on to her website." "That must be a great comfort for you," I said.

Scene Four

I couldn't avoid it indefinitely. We'd ignored all the knocking and the notes; we'd left the phone unplugged. But finally she caught me getting out of the lift. "Oh, Jude," she gasped. "That's never crimplene?" I have to say it was an odd and rather inadequate greeting after twenty years, but I let it pass, although I couldn't help thinking a hundred-pound haircut ought to improve one's appearance rather more than hers was doing.

"Bev," I said, "what a surprise. I'm afraid I lost your numbers. But I thought you'd probably call again if it was urgent."

A pause. I assumed an expression of innocence, and challenged her to defy it. She took that challenge.

"I did call again, Jude."

"Really?" I said.

"Yes."

"We must have been out."

"I called twenty-seven times over a four-day period."

"Good heavens. We must have been out a lot."

"I also put a note through the door."

"That was you?"

"Look, Jude, I feel you've spent the last four days deliberately avoiding me."

"That's rather an arrogant way of looking at things, don't you think? Daddy and I have been busy, that's all. None of us leads our lives for other people, you know."

If she had been anticipating a pleasant expedition down Memory Lane, she wasn't getting one. In the end, we went to Starbucks for a cappuccino but I kept my guard up. I watched her at the counter, in her sharp leather jacket, moleskin trousers and knitted silk scarf in shades of dove and lilac. Italian shoes, high heels. Unnaturally flat stomach. I thought, who's colluding with the enemy now, then, eh? "You never cut your hair!" she said, brightly, as she plonked the cappuccinos down. "Well observed," I said, flicking it over my shoulders. "I have to say, I hope you don't mind, but whoever cut yours seems to have done it out of spite."

She didn't say anything. Stirred her coffee. She struggled with some kind of emotion. I scooped off the chocolate and ate it. I tried not to imagine how I looked to her, in the poncho I crocheted during free periods in the sixth form. She stirred her coffee again. This was getting rather tiring.

"I haven't seen your mum recently," I said, at last. "She all right?"

Bev's face crumpled. Evidently this was not the safe conversational area I had expected it to be.

"Oh no," I said.

She put her hand on mine, and her lip started quivering. "That's why I –. She died, Jude."

Suddenly there was a flurry of handbag activity as she found a tissue and pressed it to her face.

"Oh Bev, I'm sorry," I said. And I meant it. Despite all the boasting about Bev, I really admired Bev's mum. You'd never get Daddy surfing the net to find out what I was doing.

"They called me back from a book tour. Can you imagine? I was in ... I was in CHICAGO!"

Evidently the location was significant, although I couldn't see why. If she hadn't been in Chicago, she'd have been in Tel Aviv, or Edinburgh, or Paris, or somewhere else.

"I wasn't here! I just can't stand it that I wasn't here!"

"Bev," I said. "That's such a silly thing to reproach yourself with."

"Is it?" she sniffed.

"Of course," I said. "Let's face it, you were NEVER here."

"Jude, I've wasted my life, sacrificed it to fame and success! I've got to change everything!"

She clutched my hand and made gagging, snuffling noises into her tissue. "I'm going to change my life, Jude."

I saw now why she had sought me out. Not to gloat. She wanted me to endorse a new, caring non-working Bev, to make her feel better. Well, as Charles the First's best mate the Duke of Buckingham apparently used to say, "No way, José."

"I want to be like you," she said. "Give myself to the people I love. It's the most important thing to do with your life."

Just then, a woman came up and said, "Are you Beverley Brayfield?"

Bev wiped her nose and admitted she was.

"I just wanted to say I loved your book, what was it, *Bodice Rip*?"

"*Bodice RIP*," Bev corrected.

"Yes, of course, *Bodice RIP*! I just wanted to say it changed my life. I left my husband, took up taekwondo and got a siamese, and now I'm doing PR for a pharmaceutical giant. So thank you. Thank you. Thank you. She's very good, you should be proud," the woman said to me, touching my arm, assuming I was Bev's granny, I suppose; in any case, assuming I wanted to be impressed by the adoration Bev could elicit from a gullible, unethical cat-loving bolter with obscure martial arts interests.

"I suppose that happens all the time," I said.

"All the time and all over the world," said Bev, starting to sniff again. "And it's all worth nothing, you see, because I was in, I was in –"

"I know, I know," I said. "You were in Chicago when your mother died. Look. Do you mind me asking, Bev? How was Chicago apart from that?"

Scene Five

I wouldn't say it was a major issue, but this business of sitting and waiting for my hair to dry every day has caused the odd irritation in the twenty years I've been "giving myself" to Daddy. He's bought me eleven hair-driers of different designs, and he never misses a chance to say, "Now THAT would suit you, Judykins," when a short-haired woman appears on the screen. His favourite film performance of recent years, to judge by his enthusiasm, is Demi Moore in *GI Jane*, closely followed by Sigourney Weaver in *Alien*. Which is why, I suppose, when he said, "Your old friend Beverley has a nice sharp little haircut," at lunchtime today, I was so used to ignoring the trichological jibe that it took me a while to grasp what he was really telling me.

Bev had been round. Of course. Bev feels guilty about her own mother; she decides to muscle in on Daddy. I kept thinking of this terrible expression Mag used to throw at Daddy – "In like Flynn"; "I suppose you were in like Flynn?" she would yell. Bev had been in like Flynn. Looking round, I saw the extravagant box of chocolates on the sideboard and a bunch of lisianthus in the sink. Bev's mother had once said Bev never came without flowers. It was her code for daughterliness. And now she had transferred the code to Daddy.

I couldn't ask. But I didn't have to.

"She's a lively one," said Daddy, as I served the lunch.

I helped him to some rice. I tried to sound casual. "How long did she stay?"

"Not long."

I looked around the flat, imagining how Bev must have seen it. According to the style sections of the Sunday papers, Bev had a loft in Clerkenwell and a cottage in the South Downs. And here we were with our sixties G Plan with the split cushions; the net curtains; the old tinny record player; the gas fridge; the Trimphone. Years' worth of newspapers stacked in the hall. I could imagine her making notes. I could imagine her whirling through the mess like Tinkerbell crossed with a miracle household cleanser, brightening the flat and beguiling Daddy with stories of being successful in the big wide world.

"I wish you hadn't let her in, Daddy."

"Well, I'm sorry about that, dear, but we don't lead our lives for other people."

"No," I said.

"Did she say anything about me?"

"Yes. She said she was worried about you. She thought you needed to get out more. She said she was shocked by what a frigid little martyr you've become."

He ate the rest of his lunch in silence, carrying on with the crossword. And perhaps it was just the shock but I thought, oh my God, I've lost him. I've lost my Daddy. Beverley Brayfield has just tiptoed in here in her classy Italian shoes, passed judgement on me, and stolen my Daddy's heart.

"Dissident," he said.

[*Upset*] "What?" I said.

"Are you crying?" he said. He wasn't looking.

"No."

"You know I hate people who cry?"

"Yes."

"Non-conformist Norfolk town I make an impression on. 'Diss' 'I dent'. Non-conformist – dissident. It means your 'Paddled' is right."

I pulled myself together. Big breath.

"I'm thinking of having the phone disconnected."

"We've been through this, Judith. Dr Salmon says we need the phone."

I took his plate to the sink.

"Who do you call when I'm not here, Daddy? Is it a woman?"

I had my back to him. I was shaking. I sounded like Mag.

"That's right. It's a woman. And it's private. You have your admirers, I have my admirers."

"Except I don't have admirers," I said.

"Then more fool you," said Daddy. "That's what comes of spending half your life drying your hair."

Later, after Daddy's nap, I made us a cup of tea and switched on *Watercolour Challenge*. They were painting a really beautiful scene at an old abbey somewhere, with water and birds. You could feel the freshness of it. The sun came out; there was even a rainbow. And Hannah Gordon looked lovely in a pink jacket which Daddy loyally said was a colour that would suit me, too. That was his way of apologising, and I accepted it. He didn't even speculate about the Winnebago activity that gave her such rosy cheeks. He didn't mention her chestal splendours. I waited for the adverts before I raised the subject again. I knew it would be for the last time.

"Did Beverley leave very quickly?" I said.

"Yes, she did. In considerable haste, I think you could say."

I opened the biscuit tin and handed it to him. I'd put in some bourbon creams and some fig rolls, just like the ones we used to have from Victor Value when Daddy came home from the stall. The ones that Mag never liked.

"Ah, fig rolls," he said.

"Why did she leave so quickly, Daddy?"

"No sense of humour."

"Really?"

"Prude."

"Yes?"

We watched an advert about how easy it was to sue people for accidental injury.

"Judy, all I did was compliment her on her figure and she walked out."

I smiled. "Daddy!"

"What do you mean?"

"What words did you use? Did you say, 'I compliment you on your figure, Beverley'?"

"Not exactly."

I laughed. I was cheering up. We wouldn't be seeing Bev again, that was for sure.

"You didn't touch her?"

"No!" His outrage wasn't genuine. He winked at me. "She moved too fast."

Happy, I dunked a fig roll in my tea, and waited just long enough for it to soften without falling in. I watched Daddy as he did the same. Then we each took a bourbon cream and did it together. Synchronised dunking, the result of years of practice. Sweet and chocolatey synchronised dunking with the curtains drawn and really good telly just about to restart in the middle of the afternoon.

"Beverley Brayfield feels all guilty because she was in Chicago when her mother died," I said, offering him the biscuit tin.

"Silly tart," said Daddy.

The Married Man

JIM is an attractive, charming and slightly dandy-ish
American who has been living in London for twelve years
with his New Yorker wife Elaine. He is a successful and
famous mystery writer, and they live well in Notting Hill.
They have a child of eleven, known as Teddy. As a writer,
Jim is not at all interested in crime, only in revealing
the solutions to mysteries he has himself invented. As a
compulsive philanderer, he is routinely disloyal to his
wife, in the belief that he's too clever to be detected. He is
awesomely shallow and loves to talk about himself, but he
is really quite a nice guy; in the end we love him and feel
sorry for him for being such a dupe.

*Scene One: sound of electric whisk in bowl; Jim is humming
contentedly as he whisks some egg-whites to some nice operatic
aria in the background; he has to pitch slightly over the sound
of the whisk*

It's a writer thing, you see. Basically a writer thing. Oh.
Wait. [*The whisk stops. Panic*] That's not a piece of shell in
there? [*Relieved*] No, no, I'm fine. Do you know, I must tell
Elaine: I LOVE this new apron, I love it. It's very ... chic. [*The
whisk starts again; he sighs happily; he's doing such a good job*]
Anyway, it's a writer thing, you see, call it "omniscience".
Sometimes when you're with someone, the situation
has all the predictability of, well, um – [*looks round for
an analogy, and goes for the nearest*] all the predictability of
beating egg-white until it forms soft peaks. "Now YOU are
the photographer," I say to this girl this morning when
I open the door – and what can she say? Bingo. [*As if a
bit overwhelmed by him*] "And you must be Jim [*with British
pronunciation*] Dance, celebrity author of the Jack Scrolls
mysteries." Putting down a heavy camera bag on our
top step, she holds out a plump young luscious hand for
shaking, and I know straight away. I KNOW.

[*Whisking stops; he's immensely pleased with his soft
peaks*] Soft. Peaks. Just look at those, will you? OK, next
fold in the mixture – but not yet. First, you got to let it
rest. Watch it sweat, watch it swell. Make it think you're
through, when in fact you've only just got started. Oh yes.
Now – [*Slow,sensuous folding of mixture into egg-whites; just
occasional clink of spoon on bowl*] see how gentle this is? You
are in such safe hands here, baby. That's right. [*Ecstatic
soufflé-mix acting*] Oh, oh. [*Sighs*] O-o-o-o-oh.

I should explain about the photographer. Now, look,
forgive me if I leap ahead sometimes; the omniscience
of the writer is a gift that can also be a burden. You see,
when you know the whole story before it starts; when
you can see how every aspect of it will play, sometimes
you are tempted to skip preliminaries. And that's a big
mistake. [*Businesslike*] So. They do this every five years or

so. The publishers want an "author pic". So what can the poor author do? – I mean, besides getting a haircut and manicure and arranging his Ellery Queen statuettes on the Bechstein? Also, in my own case, humbly adding his Poirot Prize, his Golden Deerstalker and his Best-Dressed Man awards. Elaine always goes out when author pic time comes round. She leaves me here alone with a young female photographer! She even says, "Have fun!" Oh, Elaine, she's been married to a leading mystery writer for the past fifteen years; she is so smart she guessed the twist to *The Sixth Sense* in the first eight minutes; but where my romantic life is concerned, she never suspects a thing. Laura, this girl was called. "Is your wife home?" she asks as she enters. "What a magnificent hallway." "Mrs Dance is playing tennis," I say, taking her coat. "The housekeeper is at Harrods. My daughter Teddy is away at school. So it's just the two of us. I call that cosy."

[*He samples some of the mixture*] Man. Am I good or am I fabulous?

Laura, I have to say, is gorgeous. We arrange ourselves in the first-floor lounge. She says the light from the floor-to-ceiling windows is perfect. And, what a good girl, she asks questions. [*As girl*] "So Jack Scrolls is –?" I explain, patiently, that he's a sophisticated, Ivy League amateur detective in the great tradition of mystery writing. [*As girl*] "As opposed to –?" [*It's an innocent inquiry, but he's always a bit touchy about other types of crime writing; his voice rises*] I said, "As opposed to the lonely, morally frail, jazz-besotted policemen with collapsing marriages everyone else writes about!" [*Recovers from outburst*] I'll pop this in now.

[*Oven door is opened and baking tin placed on shelf*] Eight minutes.

[*He sets wind-up timer then sits down, very pleased with the job done; drinks coffee during next bit; there is a tick-tick-tick faintly until the "ping" at the end of the scene*]

She's seen me on TV, but she's never read me. But that's fine, fine – fine. I never tire of talking about Scrolls. You see, he holds the key to the mystery of the human heart, yet at the same time he's just – well, a regular American guy with a nice, simple two-syllable name, some great dental work and an unbeatable collection of vintage brogues. I made his home town Socrates, Connecticut – but I have to admit this pleasing classical allusion just sails over the heads of the dime-store fans. And he has a popular sidekick called Buddy who says things like, [*Marx Brothers-type voice*] "We got the what, boss; but we don't got the why." I based Buddy on my own father, incidentally. He was horrified. "What makes Jack Scrolls special," I explain to Laura, "is that first he looks at what's there. Then he looks at what ISN'T there. That's what makes him infallible."

[*Slightly mocking*] "Infallible?" she says. "No one's infallible." I smile. What does she know? She switches on one of her lights. It's bright. "So how long have you had this fabulous house?" I tell her we borrow it from my billionaire publisher, Sir Edward Palliser – of Palliser Press. I explain this is quite a regular arrangement. When Elaine and I moved to good old London town, twelve years ago, Ted (well, WE call him Ted; you would call him Lord Palliser of Holland Park) offered us this house rent-free! Lucky he's such a fan of Jack Scrolls, because he also pays Teddy's school fees, and takes Elaine to the Frankfurt Book Fair for three weeks each July, because [*it's a family joke*] she's such a fan of the hot dog!

[*Drinks coffee*] The rest is run-of-the-mill. An author pic works best if you can see the person's hands. It's a trust thing. Also, I paid twenty pounds for the manicure, so I'm not about to waste it. I lean on one hand. Flash. I fold both hands under the chin. Flash, flash. Throughout the shoot, she moves around, adjusting the camera, swivelling lights. Is Jack Scrolls married? No. Am I like Jack Scrolls? Well, Laura – Flash! – that would be telling. Flash, flash, flash. Why hasn't there been a TV series based on the Jack Scrolls books? I say that's a strange question, and she says, "Not really. Detective books are always being adapted for TV." [*This is a touchy subject*] I say there's been a whole heap of interest in Scrolls for TV, as it happens, but that I don't want to jeopardise the integrity of the books by handing over my characters to people who won't respect them. "Really?" she says. Flash, flash. "So Lord Thing of Thing doesn't actually live here with you and your wife?" [*Uncomfortable; rattled*] No, I say. Why should he?

Well, it's time to assert control. Less exposition, more action – if you'll forgive me for getting technical. So I say, with a big smile, "Laura." And she says, "Mr Dance?" I say, "Laura, now that you've taken so many pictures of me – why don't I take a picture of you? [*Beat. A little laugh*] "No, no," she protests. [*He loves this memory; revels in it*] "Oh come on," I say, reaching for the camera. [*Gentle*] "What could you be scared of?" I say. "This is fun, Laura. You're lovely. And if I may say so, in all modestly, I'm pretty lovely too." I wait. This is the crucial moment, the best. This is what life's all about. This is life reduced to its essence. This woman can walk out right now, or she can stay. She doesn't appear to be walking.

"What about your wife?" she says. Bingo. I put my hand through my hair, which – I just happen to know this – makes me look super-adorable, and take the camera. She sits on the sofa, arranging her skirt. She's self-conscious and blushing. It's great. "Look at those ankles," I say. I press the shutter. Flash. "Now. Show me your hands." She laughs; she's embarrassed, but she is not saying no. She is not saying stop. "Put your hand to your neck, honey. Here. Oh, that's beautiful, beautiful." I help her place it at an elegant angle to her throat, then kneel in front of her, very close. She shuts her eyes, but that's OK. "Perfect," I say. I take fifteen shots before I speak again. "Open your eyes, sweetie."

[*Pause ... Last tick-tick-ticks then "Ping" from the timer*] Bingo. And when Elaine gets back from tennis two hours later to find me loading the dishwasher, you know what? The same old story. [*Very pleased with himself*] She doesn't suspect a thing!

Scene Two: sound of Gaggia machine making an espresso

[*He is angry, but holding it in to start with*] So I was having a good morning, as it happens. [*Clunk of cup on saucer*] *Foot and Shoe Monthly* arrived in the post and that's always a red-letter day. Plus I just always feel kind of optimistic in the spring. Jack Scrolls mysteries being "Christmas reads" according to Ted, spring is the time for checking off the proofs of one book and then getting down to the next, which is already planned in some detail, of course, [*starts to lose it*] though I don't know why I should bother, I DON'T KNOW WHY I SHOULD BUST MY ASS, WHY DO I BUST MY FRIGGING ASS WHEN THEY SEND ME CRAP LIKE THIS?

[*Swigs coffee and reacts to how strong it is, possibly by coughing*] A new copy-editor, they say. Clare without an "i", a specialist in "crime writing" – although how many times do I have to tell them I'm NOT a crime writer, I write MYSTERIES. [*Rustle of paper*] She's discovered a few "inconsistencies" in *A Brush Dipped in Death*. She has some "queries". Of course I can over-rule this Clare-without-an-i; that's my author's prerogative; but maybe I OUGHT to turn my attention, they say, to the scene when Jack Scrolls – and we're talking about JACK SCROLLS here, that's what gets me, the guy's frigging INFALLIBLE – it's the scene when Jack Scrolls is inspired by the Riddle of the Sphinx to realise that the whole mystery turns on the victim's missing walking stick. [*Deep breath*] OK, I need to explain. *A Brush Dipped in Death* is set on a beautiful, unnamed Greek island. An elderly member of a British painting group is found dead in the harbour. Did he maybe lick his paintbrush and swallow cadmium yellow (which is deadly poison if you didn't know)? The local police are baffled. And since it's Easter, the Greeks are busy slaughtering lambs and exploding religious fireworks, so there's blood and dynamite all over the place, contaminating the crime scene more than somewhat. By chance, Jack Scrolls arrives at the island to examine a religious icon on behalf of the Metropolitan Museum in New York, and finds himself intrigued by the mystery.

Now, also by chance, and this new editor says it's way too much of a coincidence, at breakfast one morning on his sunny terrace, Scrolls dips into his *Larousse Encyclopedia of the Ancient World* (and he ALWAYS has Larousse in his pigskin portmanteau; anyone who reads my books would know that) and spots the entry on the Riddle of the Sphinx – and from that he figures the whole thing out. Now, I don't want to get technical here, but it goes without saying that the whole book, the whole damn book, is built on this epiphany; this moment of almost divine revelation. But is epiphany good enough for Miss

Can't-Even-Spell-Her-Own-Name? No. She says this is "not proper deductive method ... Absence of real clues cheats the reader ... If this is typical of Jack Scrolls, no wonder these books are never adapted for TV."

[*Worked up*] Elaine was out. She was out before I woke up this morning. She'd told me last night she was going to John Lewis to meet a friend, and we have this arrangement that we call each other only in an emergency, out of respect for the importance of my creative process. But I needed to talk! I tried Ted, but he wasn't in his office; they said he'd gone to Paris "for lunch", if you can believe that. So I was just fuming over this stupid letter, when the photographer from yesterday rang. "Hi, Jim!" she said, and I said, [*agitated, but attempting to sound cool*] "Oh, hi," and she said, by the way, she had checked up about the Frankfurt Book Fair and it isn't three weeks in July; it's a week in October. So I said, [*as if he knew this already and doesn't understand why she's mentioning it*] "Oh, OK." I thought she might be getting stuck on me, calling so soon, so I started making my caring-husband speech about how it would kill Elaine if she knew I were unfaithful, not that I'd EVER betrayed her before, because I love her too much – when she interrupted and said there was something that might be important: she may have left an ear-ring in the bed. "YOU MAY HAVE LEFT AN EAR-RING IN MY MARITAL BED?" I said. She said, yes, sorry. "YOU MAY HAVE LEFT A MASSIVE CLUE FOR MY WIFE TO FIND – IN MY MARITAL BED?"

Well, I raced up to the bedroom and searched for it – under the pillows, under the bed. I just couldn't help thinking: what if Elaine found it already? What if that's the real reason she set off so early this morning, when she was only going to W1? What if she was leaving me? We have such a nice LIFE! I love this life! But there was no sign of that frigging ear-ring! I grabbed the bedside phone and dialled Elaine, then realised I wouldn't know what to say, so I hung up. Do you know what I was like in that mad five minutes? I was like a weak panicky person, panicking! I even chewed my nails! And then, a moment later, the phone rang, and – well, [*desperate*] WHAT THE HELL IS GOING ON?

[*Trying to work through it logically*] The caller-ID came up as "INTERNATIONAL", so I thought, "Well, that's not Elaine; she's in Oxford Street," so I lifted the receiver – and – [*confused*] it WAS Elaine. She said, "Hello? Did you call, Jimmy, dear?" I didn't speak. Then she was a bit muffled, as if covering the phone, and said, "Oui, merci, monsieur, avec du sucre." Then there was a burst of accordion music and I heard TED's voice saying, "Elaine, darling, what are you doing, are you mad?" What on earth does any of it MEAN?

Scene Three: he is flat, unhappy; it is late the same evening; late-evening music; he's had a drink or two; he sips a drink occasionally

Elaine called at five. She said she'd had a wonderful day shopping in Oxford Street with her old friend Beryl (Beryl!) and would be home around eight. She'd bumped into Ted – well, what do you know? – so he would be dropping her off. I didn't bother to cook, even though I'd planned a salmon soufflé with snow peas and my famous seared broccoli. I was just too agitated. Sure enough, at nine, there were the lights of Ted's Bentley; the slam of car doors; the tip-tip-tip up the steps. Then she swung in, looking [*upset*] so fresh and pretty, festooned with elegant tiny Parisian carrier bags, with a new diamond bracelet dangling on her wrist. "That's a nice piece," I said. "Yes!" she said, as she flung herself down on the couch and her passport slipped out of her pocket. "Isn't it convincing? It's only imitation. I got it in the costume jewellery department at Debenhams. Twenty-two fifty." She reached out and put a handful of change in the bowl on top of the Chinese cabinet, and there were some Euros and little green Metro tickets in it.

She didn't seem to notice I was quiet. It was horrible. I had to say something, I had to say, "Elaine, I know you're lying to me!", but I didn't, because just as I was preparing to speak, she presented me with this stupendous gift: a pair of immaculate coffee and cream brogues in the original Church Brothers box with an authentication certificate in French to say they once belonged to the Duke of Windsor. Look at them. [*Upset*] They're so beautiful! They are pearls beyond price! "The man said they were the Holy Grail of shoes," she laughed, "but I wasn't sure if he was being sarcastic." I couldn't speak. "I couldn't resist them," she said, kissing my forehead. "Nothing's too good for my genius husband." [*A brave squeak*] "And you got these in Debenhams, darling?" I said. She nodded. "Yes. It's amazing what you can get in Oxford Street these days."

She went to bed. I said I'd stay up and try on the brogues. And now, and now – [*trying to make light of his confusion; a laugh?*] I don't know what to think! I mean, it's crazy. It's as if she's having an affair with Ted! But she CAN'T be having an affair with Ted, because if she was, well, for heaven's sake, I'd KNOW. And they both love me. And all this. [*Upset*] All this! All this wonderful life – CAN'T be built on a LIE.

[*Sniffs, pulls himself together; the affair is impossible, and he can prove it; the effect of looking at pics of himself is to cheer him up, of course*]

Look, I've been studying this photo album. And in all these pictures, over all these years, we look so happy, the three of us. One for all and all for one! Here's the wedding day in Connecticut, just after I'd finished that little fling with Elaine's sister Carol. Oh, look how debonair I am; it's so true that good tailoring never dates. [*Suddenly remembering his task*] And you see – there is no sign of anything between Ted and Elaine in any of these. Look. [*He starts to look at more pics*] The party for the first Jack Scrolls book, the night I met Elaine. [*Excited*] That's the cake with the Scrolls credo. "First, you look at what's there; then you look at what's NOT there." I made that cake! It took me three days to frost it!

It was Ted who first introduced me to Elaine that night, of course. I remember he said, "Look out, James, she's a smart one! She'll run rings round you so fast you won't even see the blur!" [*Laughs, happy*] There's Elaine at the party. [*Looks more closely*] Oh no, it's someone else. She was definitely there, though. And Ted made a speech, but he must have gone off somewhere as well. [*Turns another page*] Here's the house in good old overcast London, with Elaine showing off her bump. Ted must have taken these. [*Not interested because he's not in them*] I don't know where I am. Oh and here – [*instantly consoled by pic of the child*] Oh. The birth of Teddy. I bought that tie specially. Our little miracle. We really showed those "experts". They tell you, "Mr Dance, I'm afraid your sperm count is simply unviable," but, I ask you, what do these people KNOW?

Scene Four: A "ping" of the timer; he's in the kitchen again, baking something for the next day's breakfast; radio station in background, but a late-night feel. He is very tired; it's over; but it should be ambiguous whether he's relieved or depressed

It's over. What a day. Let's see how these little beauties turned out – [*Opens oven door and removes tray of something. Sniffs*] Perfect. First things first, OK? [*Drinks coffee*] I found the ear-ring. It seems Elaine found it yesterday, and slipped it into an envelope for Mrs Holdsworth. I discovered it propped against my new Italian espresso machine! I think she wanted me to see it first, but of course I can't be sure. [*Reads note*] "Mrs Holdsworth, is this yours? Since I found it on the bedroom floor, there can be no other explanation for it getting there." She's underlined that part. "Please make sure Mr Dance is not disturbed while working today. His talent is so precious to us all." [*More reassured than he ought to be*] Well, that's a nice thing to say, anyway. You know what I was beginning to suspect? I mean, blame my over-active deductive mind, but I had honestly started to entertain the idea that, well, Elaine knew all about my little dalliances; but because she was having an affair herself, she didn't care!

She cared about that letter from Miss Smartypants Copy-Editor, though. When I told her, she said, "Leave this to me, dear; I'll talk to Ted." I said, "That woman really upset my idea of myself; she said you can't have infallibility as a character trait!" And Elaine said, "You're a genius, Jimmy. Some people just can't cope with that." But after she'd gone, I thought, well, if there is one way to justify Jack Scrolls's deductive method, it's to use it myself. Look at what's there; look at what isn't there. So

I made a list of everything I've learned, or realised, in the past twenty-four hours.

One. The Frankfurt Book Fair is shorter than – and at a different time of year from – what Elaine and Ted have told me for the past twelve years. OK.

Two. Our daughter is named after Ted, and has the same red hair, but we've always laughed about that, and Elaine has any number of tawny cousins in Wisconsin. So.

Three. Elaine and Ted often go missing at the same time, sometimes to Paris for lunch.

Four. She tells barefaced lies to cover up such trips.

Five. This morning she wrote to the insurance company to insure the diamond bracelet for thirty thousand pounds, and when I said, "I thought you said it was a cheap thing from Debenhams", she said, "Yes, but burglars wouldn't know that, would they?"

I sat in my den for three hours, doodling and nodding to myself, reaching my conclusions, until it got quite dark. The *Larousse Encyclopedia* method, I ought to report, was worse than useless, but we'll skip over that. Then, when Elaine got home, inevitably with Ted in tow, saying, "Look who I bumped into at the club!", I called them into the drawing room, where I had made a fire. It was a classic setting for a denouement. I'd drawn the curtains and arranged the furniture so that Elaine and Ted would have to sit in high-backed chairs beside the hearth while I leaned on the mantel and gave them the benefit of my lengthy cogitations. I had decided to start with a solemn, "I know," and watch their guilty faces while I toyed with my Marlowe Medal in the firelight. So it was a bit annoying when, the moment they came in, Ted switched on the main lamps and moved the chairs back to their normal places. I always forget that, as far as Ted's concerned, this is his house.

"Look, James," he said. "Sorry about that copy-editor bitch. Whatever Jack Scrolls does is what Jack Scrolls DOES. You know that; I know that; your dear devoted fans know that. She didn't know it, she's out on her arse, you're a genius, what's for dinner?" He helped himself from the sherry decanter and poured one for Elaine. She said, "Thanks, darling," and curled up on the couch to sip it. This wasn't precisely the mise-en-scène I had envisioned, but it would have to do. I prayed to Jack Scrolls to get me through.

"I know," I said, quietly. And for a moment, I had them exactly where I wanted them. It was like something out of Terence Rattigan. Ted, who had been tinkling at the piano, gently closed the lid and said, "What did he say, darling?" Elaine looked at him meaningfully. "He said, he knows."

Now, this was more like it. This they could adapt for TV! I took a deep breath. Unfortunately, I'd forgotten to pocket the Marlowe Medal, and it would have broken the mood if I'd gone across the room to pick it up, so I steepled my fingers together instead. "Your big mistake was giving me the brogues on your return from Paris. You WERE in Paris, of course?" Elaine stopped breathing. Ted half rose from the piano stool. And I thought, I've got you. "I've been doing some thinking," I said. "And I know what you've been keeping from me. I just don't know how you thought you'd get away with it. It's quite hurtful, incidentally, to be taken for a fool." The tension was fabulous, but I could keep it inside no longer. "Elaine. Ted. It's over. I've won the *Foot and Shoe Monthly* Best-Dressed Man of the Year Award, haven't I?"

Elaine let out a laugh, and then sort of unravelled on the sofa in a great spasm of relief. I knew it. She had HATED hiding the good news. I think we were all really relieved! Hurriedly, she jumped up and put her arms round me. "It's no good trying to keep a secret from you, is it, darling?" she said, kissing my cheek and beckoning to Ted, who – after pausing only to drain his sherry glass and pour himself another – came towards me with a big smile. "Well, James, we tried to keep it a secret, but if you know, you know. *Foot and Shoe Monthly*. Yes. Indeed. Congratulations! Well done. Couldn't happen to a better-shod chap."

I explained over dinner, which was fabulous incidentally, an utter triumph, how I'd used the Scrolls method to solve the mystery, and they both said how clever I was, and how much they adored the aubergine. It's like the dog that didn't bark in the night-time, I said. If you two went to Paris and didn't tell me, it had to be BECAUSE OF ME. "Ah," they said. Once I'd realised the significance of the brogues, there was nothing to it. Ted clapped me on the shoulder and said, "It must be really something to have a mind like yours, James." And I said, as modestly as I could, that it was.

Scene Five: Epilogue

[*Whisking egg-white again; he's happy, and having to pitch over the whisk*] It was a simple process of deduction. You see – ooh, soft peaks a-coming! – a lot of the evidence pointed towards the conclusion that Elaine and Ted have been having an affair, possibly since before we were married. But a) Elaine loves me, b) Ted holds me in the utmost professional esteem, and c) it's a well-known fact that you should never trust the most obvious explanation.

[*Whisking stops. Sighs happily*] Yesterday I had lunch with Ted at his club, to celebrate *A Brush Dipped in Death*, and I admitted to him, man-to-man, that I'd had to run through the affair scenario just to satisfy myself that it couldn't be true. "An affair?" Ted laughed. "James, surely you know by now that Elaine and I share only one dirty secret, which is our admiration for YOUR WONDERFUL WORK. What have we always said? It's one for all and all for one – and you're the one, Jim. You're the one!" I said I did know that, yes I did. He said it was unfair that one man should have so much: so much talent plus such good looks, not to mention such excellent taste in footwear. [*Faux-modest laugh*] Well, that's what he said. As for the annual trip in July, he was about to explain that, but I interrupted. I wanted to tell him what I'd already deduced about that: that they went away each July because that's when I'm usually finishing a book, when I need peace and quiet, and Ted said absolutely that was the reason and sorry about the terrible alibi; Frankfurt Book Fair, indeed! It just proved, though, didn't it, what novices they were when it came to deceit? He said I was free to join them any time – they go to Venice – but he reckoned that if it was a choice between swigging boring old bellinis in Harry's Bar and giving another magnificent Jack Scrolls mystery to the world, there was only one choice good old Jim Dance could take! [*Happy sigh*] And of course, he's right. I live for my work. It is my life.

The waitress, I realised, was someone I'd spent a very energetic afternoon with last time I dined here. And across the room was a fairly well-known horsewoman who had once taken me back to her hotel in Piccadilly. I pretended not to see her, but I knew she was looking at me, so I ran my hand through my hair. Having secret knowledge like that, like the fresh memory of the soft and delectable Laura – well, it makes you feel … infallible.

While Ted signed for the lunch, I wondered aloud when the judges would be contacting me about the award, and he said that, actually, he had phoned *Foot and Shoe Monthly* this morning. Everyone at the magazine – which Ted OWNS, of course; I'd forgotten that – was really thrilled that I had won it.

I said I was sorry to appear pushy: it was just second nature in me to want to tie up any loose ends, narratively speaking.

"Well, omniscience is a burden, James," Ted said, "but you must always remember that it is also a gift." And I put my hand on his and, catching the eye of that little cutey waitress, said, "Ted. Ted. Oh, don't I know it."

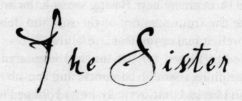

The Sister

TINA is quick in all things, and endearingly quick to laugh.

Scene One: Tina is dressing for dinner; huffs and puffs as she puts on a frock, tights, shoes etc. Remote boat engine noise. Some sort of on-board TV documentary

It's a terrible thing to say, and I know Pat will go, [*laughs*] "Ooh, hark at Tina," the way she's done since we were five years old – "Ooh, hark at Tina, Mum!" – but I was sitting on my tod this morning, on the top deck, at dawn as it happens, blimey these tights are a bit short – oof! Uff! – oh that'll do, and I suddenly realised what goes wrong on these holidays Pat and me come on. Magic mascara. [*Opens mascara*] I love you. [*While applying mascara*] I'm not saying it wasn't nice on the deck there, all by myself without my sister. I could see the banks of the deep blue lake chugging by. The sky's all mauve. Chilly, mind, I took the blanket. Downstairs they were getting the breakfast sorted. And all round, as far as you could see, there was just desert – Nubia, can you believe it, grey Nubian desert all around this lake, grey – like the colour of the stuff you see spinning round in the Dyson and think, "Blimey, where did that lot come from? I haven't got a single thing that colour." So. It was lovely. I'm not going to turn round and say I was unhappy. It was just – I know, "Ooh, hark at Tina!" – I realised it's the same old people on this boat. [*Pause*] Roasted peach lipstick, they're having a laugh. And I felt this wave of disappointment, yeah? The Waters of Nubia with the same old bunch; this dull old lot who'll be like lambs to the slaughter for Pat.

Now it's not that I dislike all this. If Pat turned round and went, Tina, why don't you take holidays on your own in mud huts in Mongolia if you dislike our trips so much, I'd go, Pat, that's not fair. I always look forward to the social side of our holidays, as for example didn't I suggest we spend a couple of evenings at my house, Pat, wrapping each other like mummies in Andrex so we could excel in the traditional Nile cruise party games? So I'm very optimistic before we set out, and even when we get to the departure lounge and everything – in fact, my problem, Pat, and it's why both my marriages have ended in muck and bullets, is I'm too optimistic about people, which leaves me susceptible to anti-climax. "Ooh," goes Pat, "hark –" Well, you know what she's like by now. But it's true. I do, I hope for too much. And then, when your beloved husband Tony turns out to be a weakling, and your beloved Marty turns out to be a drugs fiend, and everyone who's signed up on a cruise across this Nubian lake towards the great Temple of Ramses II at Abu Simbel turns out to be an ex-council tax officer from Hastings who stares at Pat with his gob open thinking she's a cross between an angel and a genius AGAIN, well, I just feel a bit let down.

Do you think anyone'll notice I've made a right dog's elevenses of my hair? See, here I am dressing up for dinner, knowing Pat will be blowing everyone away, including me. Why can't there be people on these boats who can blow Pat away? Just once would be nice. The contrast with the places brings it all home, as well. I mean, it's all right obviously for someone to be a dull bloke with thick specs and two watches on the same wrist who used to be a structural engineer, just so long as he's not with you on the great plain of Giza looking at the Sphinx being boring, or tracing the walls of the ancient site of Troy being boring. Pat doesn't mind. My sister doesn't take the interest in the ancient world that I do. Say the name Homer to Pat and she goes, [*impersonates Homer Simpson*] "Doh!" Although I have to say she brought a CD last week of the Bangles singing "Walk Like an Egyptian", which is a lot more than she usually does by way of research. But the thing is, Pat comes on these things mainly just to dazzle the plebs. I feel awful saying it, but it's true. She'll be wearing the gold outfit this evening. She'll have used that glittery stuff on her eyes. And once she shows them her medal, they'll be putty in her hands. "Nineteen seventy-six?" they go. "Munich? Moscow?" "Montreal," goes Pat. "Got your medal, Tina?" She loves being a celebrity. It doesn't bother her she's a celebrity who isn't rich or even very famous. Watching it dawn on people that they OUGHT to know who she is – that they faintly, faintly remember who she is – makes it somehow even better.

[*Lights cigarette, and smokes during next bit*] At least Pat's glamour gives them something different to talk about. Otherwise it's all a bit drastic. Comparing notes on other cruises; [*hifalutin voice*] "You didn't see Petra? Oh, but you must see Petra!" And then there's the ones who spend half their lives going on things called "In the Wake of the Conquistadors" and "Jewels of the Baltic" just so they can say afterwards they don't think much of them. You hear the same things over and over, an' all. "You are the weakest link, goodbye." Guarantees a laugh every time. "You are the weakest link, goodbye." [*Exhales*] Oh, and they always tell you they're squandering the kids' inheritance – even if you get in first with, "I bet these good people are taking their kids' inheritance, Pat, and squandering it," they still say it! They don't get the hint! "You guessed!" they go. "That's what we say to the kids, we're squandering your inheritance!" [*Groan*] It shows you where the money is. The missing millions. There's the pink pound and the grey pound, and then there's this unbelievably tedious kids'-inheritance-squandering pound you don't hear half enough about.

[*Finishes fag*] I'll shut up about it. Pat will be chomping next door. All dolled up. She's got her eye on the courier as usual. Hisham. "I wouldn't push him out of bed," she goes, quite loudly, when we're on the bus from Aswan Airport at midnight, each clutching a wilting single rose, and all sweaty and exhausted and horrified by the way the natives snatched our bags from the carousel and then demanded stinky Egyptian money we didn't have yet. I just hope I don't have to sit next to Kevin again from last night. That was so out of order. "Janice!" he goes to his wife. "You'll never guess. These girls from Rainham paid almost double what we did, because they booked direct." I don't say anything but I give Janice a little wave, as if to say, "Your bloke's a right berk, then?" I got my own back later, anyway. Waiting at the buffet behind Kevin, I go, "I suppose you've heard it's all crap about only drinking the bottled water? See that woman over there –?" I pointed to one of the Spanish group we don't mix with. "She told me, straight up, she saw them pulling water out of the lake and putting it in these bottles." With any luck the tap water should lay him up for several days, if not actually kill him. Boring people often die on cruises; it's what you might call an added bonus. [*Laughs*] Which one was it when that bloke Geoff died? 'Passport to Cephalonia'? 'Voucher to Constantinople'? One of those. We had a little party. And what about when the courier died, in Pat's cabin, on that Iceland trip 'From Geyser to Glacier'! The look on Pat's face! [*Hysterical*] I said they should rename the tour in his memory, 'From Geezer to Corpse'. [*Pause*] I'm sure she'll see the funny side of it one day.

Scene Two: Egyptian music, convivial sounds. Tina is in shock, doesn't know whether she's pleased or not; very agitated

Well, it didn't take long for Pat to tell the Olympics story, did it? Good old Pat. Broke her own record, I should think. Someone must have asked if I was her maiden aunt, as usual, coz she suddenly goes, quite loud, "No, no, Tina and me are twins! Aren't we, Tina? Surely you remember the Conway twins? Pat and Tina Conway. The Blonde Torpedoes. We were on *Jeux Sans Frontières* and everything." I could see everyone racking their brains, trying to remember. The best minds of Hendon, Gillingham, Harpenden and Halifax, addled by a day under the hot sun taking pictures of the exotic dark-skinned Nubians guarding the imposing Temple of Wadi Something or Other, now strenuously applied to going back twenty-five years to an Olympic Games in Canada that they probably didn't register much in the first place. In the end, this mousy woman Jill who has the vegetarian option and always says it's ever so much more tasty than our carnivorous one, she said, "Oh I remember. Did one of you fail a drugs test?" and we both said, "No!" "Tina and me won three swimming medals between us at the Olympics in 1976. Got your bronze, Tina?" I smiled and showed my empty hands. I gave my medal straight to Dad, Pat knows that. And Dad took it down the Fox in Billericay one night in 1977 and we never saw it again. I don't care. When you're a true Olympian you don't need to prove it. That's how it is with really big things. If you say you've got a first whatever it is degree in cleverness from Cambridge University, people don't ask to see the certificate, you know. People assume you wouldn't lie about a thing like that. Like I always say, there's no mystery how Jeffrey Archer got away with it for so long.

Sod it, I'm having a shower. [*Sounds of running water; during next bit she gets undressed and has to raise voice over bathroom noises*] So then everyone starts taking an interest. The boring Kevin, who paid considerably less than us for this holiday, remember, said all the usual things, and I thought, Pat, here we go. When you're a celebrity, you hear the same stuff time and again, and it's your duty, I think (I know, hark at Tina), to pretend these are new questions no one's ever had the wit to ask before. Kevin goes, "I had no idea you were famous." I go, modestly, "Well, it was a long time ago." Jill, the vegetarian, says, "Well, I can't remember you at all." And then Kevin goes, "I could have been a swimmer, I had very good racing turns, but I developed sinusitis." And I go, "Ah." Because people always say something like that. And there's no reply you can make. I bet Andrew Lloyd Webber meets a lot of people who could have been a knighted multi-millionaire composer if they hadn't developed sinusitis too. I bet Stephen Hawking meets a lot of people who could have formulated a revolutionary theory of time, if their Oxbridge application form hadn't been eaten by the dog. When I'm queuing up at the gates of Heaven, I'll say to St Peter, "I could have been a saint, you know, but my dad wouldn't let me use the moped."

[*Gets in shower; has to shout*] So I don't say anything to that. I don't want details of bloody Kevin's nasal problems. But then, things improve a bit when he asks where me and Pat got started, and I say, "Well, the public baths in Romford, actually," and he asks whether we teach (no, we call it coaching), whether it's an unfair advantage to have enormous feet like that Australian bloke in the Sydney Olympics (no), where we stand on all-over body suits (all in favour), and so on. Jill looks visibly bored. I blame the lack of protein. And then finally, Kevin goes to Pat, "Janice and I don't take much of an interest in the world of sport. Too busy with one thing and another." So I think, oh yeah, don't tell me. But Pat stops describing to the Gillingham people how although we were born thirty minutes apart, Tina was only ever a tenth of a second behind in the races, so she deserves a lot of credit for the way she nearly caught up, and says, "What do you do, then, Kevin?" in a very gracious way. And then Janice leans across and drops the bombshell. "Kevin's a genius in the world of graphic image-making, girls. He works with Steven Spielberg, Tim Burton, George Lucas. We've got two Oscars on our mantelpiece." [*Shower abruptly switched off*]

Kevin pretends he's a bit cross with Janice. "Oh don't, Janice," he says. "You promised. You know I'd much rather hear about what the girls do." And she goes, "What they did twenty-five years ago in Canada that no one can remember?" And he says, "Yes." But Janice, it turns out, has been dying to tell us all about this Hollywood stuff. It's been driving her nuts pretending to be impressed by swimming. "Have you been to LA, Tina?" she says, and I say, "No." "I wanted to move to LA," she goes on, "but Kevin prefers to keep the movie world at a distance, don't you, dear? Kevin says it's very superficial. Doesn't want to lose touch with ordinary people. He said this morning, didn't you, dear, we would never have met two lovely unaffected girls like Tina and Pat in Hollywood." At which point the veg-for-brains Jill suddenly caught up with the conversation. "Steven Spielberg?" she said, stretching her eyes. "Well, I don't know about the 1976 Olympics, but Steven Spielberg? THAT's famous."

I looked at Pat. She looked at me. [*Amused*] Ooh, Pat. Pat's not going to like this. As soon as I could, I went out on deck and stood on the prow and sort of hugged myself. The wish come true! Someone with more celebrity than Pat! Stars; stars in a black, black sky. [*Lights up again*] The idea was to have a bit of time to myself, but they're jumpy in Egypt about tourists getting attacked, so after about twenty seconds Hisham came on deck to bring me back in. "Don't jump, Rose!" he says. He's referring to *Titanic*, of course, which just goes to show how weird the world is. At the pyramids they wave postcards under your nose going, "Take a butcher's at these." And when you walk off without buying any, they say, "See you later, alligator." So when Hisham says, "Don't jump, Rose," I laugh and he laughs, and it's really nice for a minute. Nice bloke,

Hisham. Very patient with people like Pat who get Lower Egypt and Upper Egypt the wrong way up; who can't say Nefertiti without sniggering about the titty bit.

"Isn't this fantastic?" I say, waving at the night sky. "You are fantastic," he says. "I have been watching you. Not boastful like your sister." He leads me back to my cabin, and we're laughing about *Titanic*, and when we look in here the cabin-boys have somehow used all the towels to make a model of a striking cobra on my bed. They do it every day – sometimes a cobra, sometimes a crocodile. But I pretend it's a surprise and I scream, and he says, "I'll save you, Rose!" and he jumps on the bed and wrestles with the towels until they come apart. And I laugh and laugh. "You won't kick me out of bed, I think," he says, breathless, finally. And I think Pat's really not going to like this, but on the other hand she did kill that bloke in Iceland and Hisham's too young to die. So I shut the door softly behind me and switch off the light.

Scene Three: deck sounds, fading to cabin (air conditioning; distant chug of boat's engines); Tina is angry

Pat and I had it out this afternoon. And I'm bloody glad we did. The thing was, we arrived at Abu Simbel this morning – the thing we've come thousands of miles to see – and what does she do? She says, well, that's nice, are you pleased then, Tina, and she looks at Abu Simbel from the deck and then says she feels a bit tired and disappears to her cabin for a couple of hours, and Hisham says he's feeling a bit unwell, and I'm like thanks a lot, left trailing on my tod round this amazing place with Janice, who's like a dam's been burst, now we know how important

Kevin is, can't stop bloody going on about what she wore to the Oscars and how it suited her a lot more than it did Drew Barrymore, who was wearing the same outfit. "At the same time?" I go. "What?" "Never mind," I go. "Kevin could re-create all this for the screen, you see, on his computer," says Janice, pointing at the statue of Amun-Ra in the holy of holies. I wish Hisham had come with us. This always happens when I sleep with someone; they go all sheepish and don't want to see me again. I think I'm too keen, if you know what I mean. Whereas with Pat, she goes all not bothered, and they become enslaved.

One of the doorkeepers tries to show us around and me and Janice keep saying no thank you, no thank you, but he won't go away, so in the end I give him some money, which is the wrong thing to do as he now feels he's got to earn it, so he keeps on following us about. "Boat," he says, pointing at an outline on the wall. "Slaves." And I keep walking off, trying to work out what I'm looking at with just the aid of my little torch and my book on *How to Recognise Egyptian Gods Unaided Because You Have Bonked the Native Guide*.

I thought I'd have to pay for it with Pat. That's why she sulked all morning, I thought; she knew I'd been at the rumpy-pumpy when she hadn't. But when I get back aboard I see Hisham leaving her cabin and there she is wrapped in a bath towel having a fag with the door open and I thought holiday or no holiday, Pat and me we've got to have this out. "You look terrible, Tina," she said. "Not much sleep last night, I understand from the horse's mouth?" She always does that. Gets the boot in first. I say, "Why are you so competitive, Pat?" and she says, "Why are you such a loser?" And I go, that's better than being a show-off, and she goes, at least I'm not a bloody snob.

A what, I go. You're a snob, Tina, everyone says so. Me? A snob? How could I be a snob, I go, what have I got to be snobby about, and she goes, "That's what I'd like to know, Tina." I'm almost speechless. Everyone says so? That's so typical of Pat to say everyone says so. What she means is she's been talking about me with Hisham. She steals a bloke I really like, and I'm the one in the wrong! It's never-ending, this. "A tenth of a bloody second, Pat!" I shout. And she shouts back, as I storm out and slam the door, "Ha! Yes! A tenth of a bloody second!"

I cried afterwards. Came back in my cabin, locked myself in the bathroom and cried. [*Self-pity*] All my life I've seen people going, "Isn't it funny how those two can be so alike and so different? Pat's so outgoing! And what lovely cheekbones. Tsk, poor Tina hasn't got cheekbones at all. And Pat got the gold, too, of course, because when it came to the big day in Montreal she swam the better time." "The better time" – that's what they'll put on Pat's gravestone. "She had the better time." I'll never forget how I raised my head out of that water, tore off my goggles and looked at the clock; how my pounding heart almost broke. In my heat, you see, I broke both our records; and then in the final Pat swam in the lane next to that amazing German who got the silver and although I matched my qualifying time, they both beat me, Pat got the gold and I got the bronze. So they'll put "Pat Conway – she had the better time" on Pat's gravestone. And on mine, which will be slightly smaller than Pat's and further away from the path, it will say, "Tina Conway – pipped at the post".

It's not easy having Pat as your sister. I never beat her at anything. I should have stopped introducing my friends to her years ago, because inside of twenty minutes they always fall in love with her, and I can see this look cross their faces when they realise they've sort of forgotten what they ever saw in me. "She's amazing, your sister," they say, thinking I'll be pleased. "Can your sister come?" they ask. Look at my wedding to Tony. Pat not only upstaged me with a chic tailored outfit in contrast to my sticky-out dress, but danced provocatively with the best man, and even got in more photos than I did. The man who took the video made a short film which could have been called *A Day in the Life of Pat*. "You're the clever one," mum used to whisper privately to me, folding a stray bit of my hair behind my ear. Can you believe it, I kept that as a precious secret for about twenty years and finally, when both Mum and Dad had passed on, I told Pat one day when I couldn't think of any other way to hurt her. "Well, Mum said I was the clever one," I said, flatly, playing my unbeatable trump. And Pat wasn't hurt! Her eyes filled with tears and she said, "Oh Tina, wasn't that a kind thing for Mum to say?"

We sail back from Abu Simbel tomorrow. Pat hasn't even been ashore yet. In fact, now I come to think of it, she's hardly been ashore the whole trip. And now she's put a note under my door to say she's so upset by our argument she's not coming to dinner – so I'll have to go on my own, and it's bloody mummification night, with the bog roll, so what a waste of all that practising. Janice couldn't guess what Egyptian party games involved, so I said if she put a hook up Kevin's nose, and dragged his brain out through the nostrils, she'd stand a pretty good chance of winning. She'd get my vote, anyway.

Scene Four: Tina; sounds of deck, chugging, birds

Well, you won't believe it. Hisham's being chucked off the boat for sleeping with the tourists. Pat came knocking at my door at eight o'clock, saying, "Tina! It's terrible!" And I thought, oh no, she's killed another one, but it was that he got caught with the vegetarian in the middle of the night, and the tour company are sacking him. Pat and he had a regular early-morning rendezvous, apparently, which explains why she was so tired all the time, and incidentally clarifies that she was sleeping with him before I was, in case I ever doubted it. So she got fed up waiting, and went to have a look for him at about half past seven, and he told her what had happened. Pat was so upset I had to nurse her at the breakfast table, and get her a special boiled egg and a special cup of tea, while Jill, the erstwhile vegetarian, had a massive fry-up to restore her spirits. And when we set sail from Abu Simbel I was so preoccupied making sure Pat was all right that I forgot to watch it or even say goodbye. If I hadn't mentioned that – I only mentioned it – things might be all right now. But I said, "Oh Pat, that was the only chance in my life to see that beautiful sight, and I missed it because of getting you some soldiers," and she said, "I've decided I don't want to come on holiday with you any more, Tina." And I said, "Oh." And she said, "Sorry. I'm a bit upset." And I said, "No, no, that's all right, Pat. I was going to say it soon if you didn't." And she said, "Really?" and started crying. And I thought, why can't I say something cutting? But I couldn't. Instead I looked at her weeping over this Egyptian casanova, and I said, "Pat. I never want you to be unhappy." And she says, "I never want you to be unhappy either, Tina."

[*She's quite affected by all this. Lights up, sniffs*] I'll be all right. I just had to come back here for a bit and think. I haven't told many people this but I did therapy for seven years with this woman called Georgina and every step of the way she was saying she'd never seen sibling rivalry like it: if I was to evolve as a human being I had to shake off Pat; stop comparing myself to Pat; stop bloody going on holiday with Pat, no wonder my marriages didn't last; stop defending Pat. And I said in the end, all right, come to my house and meet Pat, I'll get her round, come on, it will help you get a handle on it. And Georgina came round and I didn't tell Pat who she was and Pat looked great and was all poised and fantastic and brilliantly well groomed and charmed the pants right off her, and I'll never forget, Georgina collared me at the front door with this manic gleam in her eye and said, "You were right, Tina. She's amazing." "So can I stop coming?" I said. "On the contrary," she said. "I think we should step it up to five times a week."

The thing is, I could break away from Pat if I wanted, that's what she didn't understand. All my life I could have turned round and gone, "Pat, stop ruining my life." I mean, I'm not stupid. Even Mum used to say, "If she makes you feel small, Tina, you've got to stop living in her shadow." But the way I see it is, Abu Simbel makes you feel small. The pyramids of Giza make you feel small. What's wrong with it? I just remember how on July 24, 1976, Pat dived into that Olympic pool and she carved through the water like a dolphin. We were in the same race but whenever I watch it, it's Pat I follow – her white hat so steady, the grace and beauty of her windmilling arms, the strength of her kick, the absolute determination to prove herself the best in the world. I look at that race again and again.

The big German girl on one side of her; me thrashing my way to the bronze in lane eight, the crowd cheering and yelling and the commentator saying, "And Pat Conway seems to be leaving the others behind!" And I never stop saying, as she forges through, Pat Conway reaching and kicking and bloody well winning, [*very affected*] "That's my sister, that's my sister, that's my sister." [*Trying not to cry*] Ooh, hark at Tina.

The Husband

ANDY is a cheerful, banal Scottish man, married for the
past fifteen years to Sarah – who has recently started to
pronounce her name as "Sara", the first syllable rhyming
with "car". They live in Ayrshire, in considerable multi-
bedroomed comfort, because his roofing business has been
very successful. She's not a trophy wife exactly; she's only
five years younger than him. But she has never worked,
and they have no children. He is in a private bed in a
large hospital, having been rushed in, suffering from
acute abdominal pain. He stays bouncy throughout.

Scene One: Andy is very uncomfortable physically; in pain; quite
brave; on a drip

[*Pain*] Ah! Ooh that's bad. That's – ooh. I feel like, like I'm
going to BURST. Oh! The nurse said, don't try to move, Mr
McKee, but – ooh. I can't reach, you see. Can't reach the

mobile. And it's nearly eleven and I need to contact – ah!
– Sara, about that meeting of hers at the university. If she
got the job I can say, "Well done, Sara!" Aagh. And if she
didn't – aagh – I can say, "Och, what an outrage! You're too
good for them, sweetheart!" But that big alarming nurse
spotted the mobile when I came in, that's the trouble.
"You do know these are strictly forbidden until after the
operation?" she said, picking it up and shaking it at me.
Agh. "Now, you don't want to get me into trouble, do you,
Mr McKee?" And I said och, nurse, what a suggestion!
Agh. Shouldn't we at least have dinner first? [*Kind*] "Yes,
well," she said. "Less of the amusing backchat. I'll just
pop this into your smart wee leather hold-all here, and
we'll say no more about it." I told her I needed to text my
wife – it was about 9.30 then – but she said, "She can find
out how you are by telephoning the ward, Mr McKee. She
does know what's happened?" [*Calling; the nurse is bustling
about*] "One of my men said he would call her," I said. "It
was all so quick. I was inspecting a ROOF. Roofing is what I
do, you see. [*His standard – very weak – joke, of which he never
tires*] Och, yes: you might say I spend my whole life OUT ON
THE TILES." Well, I like to break the ice. Even when you're
doubled in agony, you've got to make the effort.

"Look," I said. [*A wave of pain*] "Aaagh. If she does happen
to call, could you wish her luck from me?" [*Calling back*]
"You're wishing HER good luck?" she said, as she rinsed
the sink in the wee bathroom with disinfectant, wiped it
with a paper towel, and operated the big metal pedal bin,
all in one smooth efficient action. [*Proud*] "Aye, a meeting
at the university! Ten o'clock. Sara's applied for the
contract to redecorate the senior common room. Blues
and golds. Swags in saffron silk. She's been working on
the design for weeks. It's based on a room in Buckingham

Palace, I think. Or possibly the Hermitage. In St Petersburg." [*The nurse at rest*] "It's YOU that needs the good luck, Mr McKee. Listen to you, you poor wee man. Thinking about someone else's palatial swags when you're that distended you look like – [*an idea*] well, you'll have seen the film *Alien*?" [*Laughs, gingerly*] "Thanks a load." [*Querying the pronunciation*] "Sara?" she said. "Well, she used to be [*normal pronunciation*] Sarah, right enough. But everyone uses the new name now."

They'll be along in a minute with the pre-med. Nice room. Wee menu to tick for later on. My own TV and telephone. Inoffensive upholstery in easy-wipe fabric. Somewhat like a Travelodge, but with the addition of crippling pain and guaranteed secondary infection. Ooh. I feel such an idiot, being rushed in here like this. Well, it felt like WIND. And all weekend Sara kept saying, [*snappy*] "Andy, could you stop lying on the floor like that, you're confusing the dog." And I'd say, "Look, Sara, I just can't shift this wind." I said to the nurse, "But is it wind, though?" And she said, "Mr McKee, between your stomach and your – [*swingeing sharp pain*] Aaaagh! Aaagh! – you've got enough wind to blow you round the world in eighty days." She seems to be excessively interested in cinema, that woman. Aagh. I hope they didn't tell Sara before the meeting. I wouldn't want her to be worrying. Och, I wish I could reach that PHONE.

Scene Two: post op. A few days after. Beep-beep, beep-beep text message alert

[*An effort as he reaches for the phone*] Agh. At last! That will be Sara. Let's see. Yes! [*Reads*] "No nws yt. Hv lrdy rdrd slk." Slk? Oh silk. Have already ordered silk. Och, that's terrible. What a way to treat a gifted person. "R U OK." [*Touched*] Ah. You see? R. U. OK. Four letters, but how much they say! Good job I had my charger in my wee briefcase, you see! Forearmed is – forearmed, or whatever it is. I've been waiting THREE DAYS for that message: imagine if the battery had run out before it came!

[*He texts back, laboriously*] "....Dear....Sara...comma.... poor...old..you...Full stop....Did-dums...Full stop....The ....surgeon........says......the........D..I..A..R, no, delete that....try again, D..I..O...R..R, nope,.........och I know.. LAVVY......problems......will......be...over....in...a...couple..... of...weeks...exclamation mark!...I.....shant.....oops, apos- trophe......SHAN'T be....out....on....the.....TILES [*laughs*]...... for....a....while...exclamation mark!......Your.......loving....... Andy.....X...X...X...X. Send.

[*Exhausted*] You certainly get a lot of time to think, lying here like this for three days without any visitors. Oh yes. And you know what I keep thinking? I don't want to sound smug, because that's the last thing I am, but you know, I am a lucky man. I mean, yes, my body did just swell up like I was fifteen months pregnant and I nearly died. And I'll spare you all the grisly details but there was a lot of weird and wonderful lavvy action, not to mention terrible, terrible pain. But I survived it OK, and soon I'll be back to my nice modern home with five bedrooms (three en suite), to my nice, clever wife, and my nice, successful business. I'm sure if we'd had children they'd have been nice as well, but we didn't, and as I was explaining to Geena, the big nurse, not having children, well that's not nice but I can live with it. The thing is, Sara has such a lot to give to the world in terms of integrated curtain design and revolutionary cantilevered tie-backs that I can absolutely see what she means about letting other people do the breeding. "There's no shortage of bairns in the world, Andy," she says. And I say I know, I know. [*Pain*] I resist the obvious riposte that there are quite a few curtains in the world already too. Ah! But it's a raw subject with her. It's one of those subjects that are best left alone. Especially if you're a supportive spouse. What's the difference between a levitating banana and Sara McKee? One has no visible means of support, while the other's got a faithful old mutt of a husband called Andy.

Geena likes to hear about Sara for some reason. She seems INTRIGUED, as if she's never met a supportive man before. She thinks I'm a saint for agreeing not to have children when it's so clear that I'd be a fantastic dad. We had a nice wee chat yesterday when she was removing my epidural (don't ask) and trying to take my mind off it. She's a confirmed singleton, she says. [*Confidential whisper*] A lot of bad experiences, she said. I said, [*kind*] Geena, you've no idea what it is to be loved, have you, dear? You've no MODEL. And she had to wipe away a tear before saying that unfortunately it's the first rule of nursing not to fall in love with your hospital patients. "Ah ha?" I said. "Is that because the implicit power relationship makes it unethical?" I said. "Och no," she said. "It's because they're generally ill and full of self-pity, plus, statistically, they have alarmingly short life expectancy."

I didn't say this, but to be honest, it's quite straightforward being there for somebody. I don't know why everybody doesn't do it. Because there's only about four rules to master. Basically, you just say, "Yes, dear, how much would you like?" when they ask you for money; "Och no, that's terrible," when they're upset about some wee silly setback; and "Well, I'VE always thought you were much too nice to her," when they've had some tiff with their best friend. Throw in an occasional "Sara's quite brilliant, you know," when you're out together socially, and just watch the result. Of course, you can still come unstuck. The thing a man always has to remember is this: while women have a very firm idea about the reaction they require from you, you must never ask them to tell you what it is. Sounds unfair? Ah ha. It is. But the idea is: they want you to understand them so perfectly that you don't need a hint. [*Laughs*] I know! Hilarious. So if you find yourself saying, "For pity's sake, Morag! Just tell me what you want me to say, and I'll say it!" you might as well go off and hang yourself. The way they see it is: if we have to ask, it shows we don't know. OR: [*slightly unpleasant impersonation of a woman*] "It's not enough to SAY it, Andy; you have to MEAN it. Saying, 'Oh, poor baby' doesn't mean you actually care!" [*Amused at how preposterous this expectation is*] Ach, bless their fluffy wee heads.

"Look, I'm Sara's rock," I explain to Geena. "I can't expect her to be mine as well." And Geena says, "A rock, is it? In that case, I'm going to call you Rocky. *Rocky IV* was the best one, uh-huh, I'll call you Rocky Four." I've never had a nickname before. Or indeed been linked in any way to Sylvester Stallone. It makes me feel quite proud.

[*Beep-beep, beep-beep, beep-beep of incoming text. Excited*] Ah-ha! From Sara! You see? Everything's on the up. Uff. Open. [*Reads*] Well. "Thnx 4 flwrs." Well, OK, OK, I know what you're thinking. The idea ought to be that SHE sends flowers to ME. But I just sent her a wee bouquet of anemones. I got Maria to arrange it from the office, and she said, "You're too good, Andy; she doesn't deserve you," or some such thing.

[*He texts a reply*] "....Dearest.....Sara.....comma......Life....

hyphen......threatening......phase.....over......exclamation mark!.....Your.....loving.....Andy XXX." And SEND.

[*Pause. Pleased*] Rocky Four!

Scene Three: a week later. He's a bit better

Do you know, I don't think I've ever spent so long by myself as I have this past ten days. Geena's been great. Although we'd get on better, obviously, if she weren't so disapproving about my sweet wee wife who isn't here to defend herself. Geena has no idea about Sara. She has no idea what we've been through. Everything's a bit black and white for Geena. "Your wife will have been to see you, then, Mr McKee?" she says, hands on hips. "Er, call me Rocky?" I say, but it doesn't disturb her train of thought. "Not even a bunch of flowers!" she says. On Thursday I found out from one of the other nurses that this no-flowers-from-wife situation was being gossiped about right down as far as paediatrics, so in the end I hatched a plan and I got Maria in the office to order some daffs to be delivered here, and it seemed like quite a good idea, but unfortunately the card said, "To Andy, from Andy. You funny man, love, Maria," which Geena read aloud in some amusement, so that was that. I know what she's thinking: Sara's some kind of spoiled, career-obsessed, curtain-mad hussy, I'm too infatuated to notice that she's deprived me of my right to fatherhood. What sort of wife doesn't come to see her husband when he's at death's door? Well, she'd be a bottle blonde, uh-huh, I can imagine her myself. A young bottle blonde with long red fingernails, an open-topped Saab, and a mahogany-tanned personal trainer named Kevin. Meanwhile, I'm some human incarnation of sweet little Greyfriars Bobby.

In fact, Sara's only five years younger than me, uh-huh, thirty-seven, we've been married for fifteen years. She's showing her age a bit now, of course. A few wrinkles round the knees, poor thing. A bit of sagging on the neck. (*Whisper*) A little bit of cellulite. Other people don't notice, of course, and I say, "I expect your clients think you're lovely, Sara, but I'm closer to you, so I can't help spotting all the wee signs of deterioration." For example, her hair. It's just gone all dry and wiry in the past couple of years. I've mentioned it to her a few times, but she's not really taken the hint – not even when I called her "Brillo head". So the other day I bought her some special shampoo for wiry hair and I left it for her to find in the bathroom. Now, not many husbands would do that, would they?

"How old was she when you married her?" Geena asked me yesterday.

"Twenty-two," I said. "She was supposed to be in her last year at the university, but it didn't turn out that way. I put her through the rest of her university and then art school. Well, the business was going well, even then. We made a pact that we wouldn't start a family until Sara had finished all her studies, and – well, a lot of things happened, and somehow or other she didn't finish until she was thirty-two."

[*Shocked*] "Ten years? She sponged off you for ten years and then refused to have children?"

I wasn't going to explain to Geena about the amount of time everyone lost when Sara's little brother had his accident in '95. Mind you, it was still ten years in total, she was right. And it was nice having someone so vehemently on your side.

"But she's very successful now," I said. "And terribly, terribly good. So all the studying was worthwhile. I still call her Student McKee."

"Uh-huh," says Geena. "Well. I can think of better names."

Jimmy's accident still makes me angry. I suppose it always will. Sara had already started her doctorate on the necessity for a post-modern paisley when the accident happened, and although I always thought it was a rubbish idea for a PhD and that she was being very poorly advised by her supervisor, we were happy enough at that stage; we were even still thinking about children. And then little Jimmy crashed his Suzuki into a brick wall one Friday night in Stirling and everything changed. One minute I had this happy wee wife who laughed at my jokes and was, I have to say, like a kind of joyful erotic mermaid between the sheets; the next, she was just a travesty of a person, a kind of hollow black hole, a howling wraith. Now, I'm not the sort for self-pity, but it was horrible to see her change like that. Horrible. Suddenly, she's up all night weeping; she's standing in the garden, weeping; she's breaking down in the supermarket, weeping. She's getting thin and weird and snappy and even – I have to say this – quite ugly and prematurely old. "It's the shock," they told me, in an effort to console. "It will wear off in a couple of years."

I think this was when I learned to be the supportive sort I am today. Because, I know I shouldn't say it, but I was marvellous. Forget Rocky Four. I was Rocky One to Seven inclusive. I drove Sara to the hospital virtually every day for the full year it took for Jimmy to die.

I remember when the surgeon explained to me, one day while Sara was in with Jimmy, that your brain inside your skull is a soft thing inside a hard thing – like a jelly, he said, inside a biscuit tin. Now, imagine hurling that tin against a wall, he said. "Ugh," I said. "Exactly. But that's what it's like for the brain in a high-impact crash like Jimmy's." He said I probably shouldn't mention this to Sara, but I told her on the way home, because I knew it would help her; or at least it would impress on her that hanging around Jimmy's bed every day, waiting for him to wake up and say, [*a bit dazed, comically*] "Ow, my head! Where am I?" was as pathetic as it was absurd. So I learned my role in our marriage at that time, but I also learned something else: that there's a limit to what one person can do for another. Sara needed to do some of it for herself, you see; protect herself from the hurt. And she couldn't. Not even for the sake of other people. As time went on, and Sara didn't snap out of it, I said to her, do you know what you remind me of, Sara? You're like a house with the roof off, letting all the wind and the rain get in. Can't you at least do something temporary with a tarpaulin?

Jimmy's accident ruined my life. But I never complained about feeling swindled. I never said, "Is this fair, Sarah? You're not the person I married! Where did the sex go?" I'm too supportive for that, you see. I'm a very, very supportive person. But I had to do SOMETHING, so I started calling her Sara instead of Sarah, as a mark of what I'd lost. She hates it. "PLEASE call me Sarah!" But I say she can be Sarah again if – well, if she ever is Sarah again. I didn't change, though; that's the point. I made a decision about that. If I don't change, then our unhappiness can't be my fault. I am still the same loving person. Whatever she wants to do with her life, I'll support her a hundred and ten per cent. [*Astonished*] She got that job at the university, by the way. She texted me, so I called to congratulate her. I said to her, "Well, they could obviously see merit there that I couldn't, Sara" – because it was garish and awful, actually – "So well done, you. And by the way, have you tried that new shampoo yet?"

I'll never forgive Jimmy, obviously. I mean, who really bore the brunt of that sixty-mile-an-hour skid? Me. The jelly inside the biscuit tin was my happy marriage, shattered to fragments. Nothing can ever quite make up for the way she made me feel when Jimmy died. She made me feel ... irrelevant. To such a supportive person, it was a smack in the face. I remember when he finally died and she came to me with her arms outstretched and said, [*a real plea; a potential turning point*] "I feel so LONELY, Andy." And I said, "Och, so do I, Sara. So do I."

Scene Four: a few days later; he's feeling quite well and ready to go home; he sorts some papers

It's been nice doing a bit of work while I wait to go home. Maria sent me the plans for the new arena. No trouble beating McPherson's to that contract, I'm glad to say. Losers; they'll be out of business before the year's end. Of course, they gave me my start twenty years ago, but it was Old Man McPherson himself who told me there's no room for sentiment in roofing. Boil it down, he says, and success goes to whoever's got the biggest balls and the longest ladder. And let's just say I've got a very long ladder. I said to the surgeon, "Will I be able to climb on roofs after this, Dr Singh?" And he said, [*cautious*] "Could you climb on roofs before?" And I said, "Yes, why?" And he said, oh, there were so many jokers who asked after operations if they'd be able to play the violin, he was just sick of it.

I texted Sara earlier; told her to expect me home at around midday. She needs me home, I can tell that. Now she's got the contract for the university, she'll be racked with worry – will I be good enough? Will I fail? Will they see through me? – and it will be down to me to say, "Well, yes, Sara. You're not being silly. This is high risk. You could very well crash and burn. But the point is, I will always be here for you, whatever happens. Those lemon curtains you did for Holyrood were truly horrible but I didn't say a word. Not a word. I'm behind you a hundred and ten per cent, and I always will be." Thank goodness I've got some of my strength back: maintaining Sara's self-esteem requires empathy, sympathy, imagination and good sense – but above all, it requires stamina.

That's always been her problem, you see: poor self-esteem. I realised it when Jimmy died. It was like a revelation. Yes, Sara seems today like such a successful person, but inside she's secretly cripplingly insecure. I mean, just to take a recent example, when I called her about getting this new job, I asked immediately, "Have you got it in writing?" And she said, [*worried*] "No, why?" Now, any other person would say, "I don't need it in writing, Andy. I know I've got the job." But not Sara. Sara is WEAK. [*Mocking her anxiety*] "No, why? What do you mean, Andy? What have I done wrong, Andy? Andy, why did you ask me whether I've got it in writing?" So I said, "Well, it would be nice to go out and celebrate, that's all. But I'd hate for us to do that, Sara, if there's any chance that you've made a mistake. I'm just saying, wait for the letter before you get too excited. It's a good job you've got me looking out for you. Any other man would be frankly dismayed by your inability to deal with tiny doubts like that." So then she went all quiet. "Why won't you let me come and see you in the hospital, Andy?" she said, at last. "We've been through all this, Sara. You'd have been upset, that's why. And I also didn't want you here because – well, let's face it, what could you have done that would be of any use? You may be shortlisted for Scottish Soft Furnishings Designer of the Year, or whatever it is" – which she is, astonishingly – "but as a person, Sara, [*a laugh*] you can't even look after your own hair."

We have the same argument over babies, of course. [*Fresh*] "Let's have a baby," she says. And it's always said in that exact tone of voice – as if this is the first time she's ever thought of it. "Let's have a baby, Andy; I think it could make us happy." And I have to say, very patiently, look, Sara, look at it from my point of view. Look how you went to pieces when little Jimmy died. How could I let that happen again? How can I trust you not to get all emotionally ROOFLESS? She knows I'm right. She also knows that, without me – exposed to the elements, as it were – she wouldn't last a night. So in the end, she agrees with me. [*Sadly*] "Och, well, there's no shortage of bairns in the world, Andy." And I say, "You're right, Sara. Good girl."

Geena came in to say goodbye. I shall miss her, she's been like a tonic. And it's so helpful sometimes to see oneself through other people's eyes. Because it's true what Geena thinks of me. I do spend my whole life looking out for Sara; I'm an unusually dedicated man. My wife once suffered a terrible setback of bereavement, but I never stopped loving her despite her total abandonment of me. And what's my reward? Well, all I know is, I don't think she'll abandon me again.

"Hiya, Rocky," Geena said. "How's it hanging?" And she gave me an affectionate clap on the back to show she'd become quite attached to me, but was too much of a cynical confirmed singleton to show it.

"Now, remember," she said. "No climbing on roofs for another month." I asked her to remind me what I'd had again, and she said it was called an adhesion. And it's no wonder I can't remember it, when it's such a benign-sounding name. I mean, it's just another word for sticking – and sticking is a good thing, I think. There's nothing nasty about sticking. "Can I call it gastroenteritis?" I said. And she said, "Mr McKee, you can call it foot-and-mouth if you want, it'll still be your guts getting into a twist." Then she gave me a big smile and said, "It's been nice knowing you, Andy. I've never met a man so truly selfless." [*Coy*] "Och," I said. "I can't help it. Sara's just got a hold over me, you see? Between you and me, I'm like putty in her hands."

The Other Woman

*SUE is extremely tough, for reasons of necessity. She is
ballsy in several different senses of the word.*

*Scene One: Sue is at home, she's got a music radio station on. She
is very tired, a bit drunk*

You'd think if Laurence is so keen on football he'd have
phoned for news of the Mendelssohn transfer! Perhaps he
didn't hear about it. But they had a Chelsea spokesperson
on the news at lunchtime, apparently, so you'd think
everyone must have been talking about it. Even Yolanda.
Yes, I can imagine the beautiful Yolanda getting all
worked up about transfer news, pausing in the arrangement of some gigantic white lilies in a perfect vase and
saying, [*odd foreign accent; she doesn't know much about
Yolanda*] "Orenz, darlink [*"Orenz" is the way the Bedouin say
Lawrence in "Lawrence of Arabia"*], Orenz, don't you write dat

celebrity fan ting about Chelsea for football magazine; zis leetle boy ees signed for fifteen million bazoomas; why you not call and consult nice editor, Sue I tink she called is, does my bum look big in dis, Orenz?"

Well, OK so that didn't happen. But I think I actually rubbed my hands with glee. Yo, Chelsea. I've never felt happier about fifteen million good British quid being paid for a left-footed nineteen-year-old Bavarian. All day, whenever the phone rang, I was sure, [*excited*] "This will be him!" and I'd jump up and shut the office door, but it was never Laurence, and of course I can't ring him to ask him why! The agony! It was always the top floor with another last-minute half-page ad, or Jeff saying he'd found out that both *Total Football* and *Four Four Two* had Beckham covers for February, when we'd cleverly gone for Michael Owen, so well done, Sue, the Best Editor in the World. He's so supportive, is Jeff. Keeps saying how tough it is for a woman in a man's world – referring to me, you see, because he's a man in a man's world, which is relatively easy. Laurence only ever rings on Tuesdays, it's the day Yolanda sees her therapist. Speech therapist possibly. "Laurence," they say. "Orenz." "Laurence." "Orenz."

I spun it out for as long as I could, too. I even hung behind in the office when Jeff had led the subs – the Five-a-Side, he calls them – round to the Rising Sun. First I corrected a few pages and then I just sat and looked at the phone, focusing all my telepathic energy on Laurence, picturing the house in Highgate – which I have never seen inside, of course, but once happened to pass six or seven times while driving round the area – then sort of praying, "Laurence. Phone Sue, phone Sue."

I mean, I did have stuff to tell him. It seems Mendelssohn is not only someone named after a major classical composer, but a Truly Good Left Foot, an increasingly rare commodity in British football which could mark a great change in Chelsea's fortunes. The premiership has to import left feet from all over the world, you know. Left feet from as far away as China have been mentioned. Jeff's doing a feature for the March issue about how we just can't grow them at home. I say it's his reward for snogging me in the taxi after the Christmas party, but he knows I'm joking. It wasn't that good a snog! Anyway, we're going to call it "Same toes, different order". Come to think of it, Mendelssohn's toes are worth three million quid each. I wonder if he's realised that yet. Or whether it will come to him when he's paring his toenails tonight in front of *Bavaria Today*. Or when he's listening to his Deutsche Grammophon recording of *Fingal's Cave*, as I'm sure he regularly does.

But in the end it got to nine o'clock and Jeff had rung me from the pub to say my pint was getting warm, boss lady, and I finally gave up. But it was a good laugh at the pub. Stuart, our non-league expert who comes in four days a month and writes stuff about Woking as if anyone cared, he had a good one. He said, "What does the giant say to Jack when he climbs the beanstalk?" and I thought, oh no, obscene joke alert, keep smiling. "All right, Stuart," I said. "He says, 'Fee, fie, foe, fum.'" Right, says Stuart, leave out the fum and write it down. Fee, fie, foe. That's it, he says. Now write the same words twice, in any order that comes into your head. All right, I said, a bit grimly, grabbing somebody's fag packet and a pen wet from a puddle of John Smith's. What have you got, says Stuart, as the others started giggling and talking behind their hands. Oh God. I finished my pint and put down the glass with a clunk. I'd got "Fee, fie, foe; foe, fie, fee; fie, fee, foe."

And he said, "Chris Eubank's telephone number," and we all fell about laughing. Jeff offered to drive me home after the next round – he's a very sweet boy, Jeff – but I got the bus instead. The woman next to me was reading one of Laurence's books, the one that won the Whitbread Prize. A classic of magical realism. A writer of trembling sensitivity. She stopped occasionally to underline things. She was trembling a bit herself. I wanted to nudge her and say, "He is such a great guy actually," but luckily my mobile rang and I thought, "This is it!", but it was just Jeff checking I'd remembered the finance meeting in the morning, and saying he'd be thinking of me, which was sweet.

[*Makes coffee*] It's funny to think how aggrieved I was when Pickering foisted Laurence on me in the first place. All the mags and sports sections were scrambling for unlikely literary football supporters at the time; there was a lot of pressure on; we were getting desperate; blimey, when I remember how close we got to approaching Beryl Bainbridge. And then Pickering says, "Get Laurence Swann." He'd met him at some posh charity dinner and found out he was a Chelsea man, which was more than enough for Mr P the Publisher with his blue and white scarf. "You'll hate him, Sue," he said, "but I think you'll find the readers will love him." Which turned out to be one of those predictions that turned out a bit like the left foot thing – same words, different order. I ended up mad about him, while the readers truly loathe him. [*Amused*] And Jeff can't stand him. He reads Laurence's copy with his jaws clenched and tears in his eyes. "He's got Celtic and Rangers mixed up, Sue! He doesn't even understand the offside rule! The man's a complete berk." And I have to say, until I met him finally at the Football Media Dinner last summer, I not only thought so too, but mentioned Laurence Swann's intolerable berkness to Pickering at every chance I got.

But then came the fateful dinner at that big Bayswater hotel, where I'd been obliged to seat him next to me, although of course it was the usual seating plan for a sports do – boy, girl, boy, boy, boy, boy, boy, boy. Big names from the world of football milled about in expensive yet somehow awkward-looking suits. Laurence wore sea green linen and a collarless shirt and approached me looking both worried and puzzled. I suppose it must have been the out-of-context protuberances on my chest that took him aback, halfway between my neck and my waist; no one else in the vicinity appeared to possess them. "I'm Sue Tranter?" I yelled above the hubbub, extending my hand. "I invited you?" And he looked round at the ranks of tables, each groaning under the weight of booze, the place already reeking of lager, testosterone and acrid male toiletries, and drawled with an air of self-amusement, "My goodness, how VERY unlike the Booker Prize!"

And I fell in love with him. I don't kid myself he's in love with me because – well, because he's a bloke, a married bloke. And there's a few rules about relationships like this – but the main one is, if the mistress dodges past the married man's defences, a flag goes up and the ref stops play. Jeff says I just like the fact Laurence is unavailable; the other night when we stayed late at the Plough he said the trouble with me is I'm a commitment phobe, to which I said, "Listen to Kilroy, here! And I always thought you were just an anorak with a keyboard." There's a bit of truth in it. But it's because he's out of my reach in other ways that I love him. I mean, I love him for not knowing much about football, and for writing a really

stinky column about it. I love him for his weird books
– magical realism; real magicalism – whatever it is, it
seems to mean incredibly old South American women
with names like Esmerelda suddenly being able to jump
over buildings. [*She obviously hasn't read them*] Oh you know.
I love his voice. And he's just so different, so OTHER, from
all the other blokes I know. "How VERY unlike the Booker
Prize." I could never get him to do the Fee, Fie, Foe. In
fact, when I think of Laurence, I feel quite ashamed of
how much I enjoyed the Fee, Fie, Foe. Laurence has no
place in the world I live in, I know that. He sent me a
round-robin e-mail once and all the other names were
Seamus Heaney and Peter Carey and Saul Bellow and so
on. Jeff said he did it just to show off, and he was probably
right, but I told him to make a note of Beryl Bainbridge's
e-mail address, because I haven't quite given up on that
idea, if I'm honest.

And the thing is, I can hardly blame Laurence for
not studying football with more attention, can I? Not
when, on alternate Saturday afternoons, [*she's very happy
about this*] when Chelsea are playing at home, Laurence
hops off the tube a couple of stops early and comes all
guilty and sweet to see me instead! I mean, I think this
might account for that not-really-there problem that Jeff
regularly detects in his copy! And it gives a whole new
meaning to the expression "forty-five minutes each way",
I can tell you. [*Happily coarse*] Stand UP if you hate Man U!
He arrives at the flat at three, I look at my watch and blow
a whistle, and we go straight to bed. Which is where we
stay, with Radio Five on the clock radio, for exactly an
hour and three quarters, with a fifteen-minute break for
cups of Bovril at half-time!

Scene Two; sound of football commentary on radio in background

Chelsea are at Southampton today; Laurence will be in Bond Street with Yolanda. "Orenz, look at diz, I vant eet!" I thought I'd do something constructive like sort my Bovril jars into expiry date order and phone my mum. It's funny, years ago I used to have proper boyfriends I could go out with on a Saturday afternoon; I lived with Simon for twelve years, for heaven's sake; we used to go to Heal's and buy beautiful furniture and oh, you know, toothbrush mugs and fancy soap, and things like that. I can't remember the last time I dithered in a soap department on a Saturday afternoon, saying, "Isn't this lovely, darling?" and waving rose-scented Crabtree and Evelyn under my companion's nose. [*Falls into fantasy dialogue*] "Smell this lovely Bronnley lemon!" "Wow." Then we'd have coffee and go all gooey about the things we'd bought, and then go and see a really mindless film in the West End. I used to love buying things for Simon. I still see cashmere jumpers that would suit him. Whenever I see that coloured glass he collected, I still feel this urge to reach for the credit card. He used to justify buying so much of it by saying, "Of course, this is for both of us, Sue." And then, when we split up, he copped the lot, the git.

Then I got the job as launch editor of *End to End*, and from then until I met Laurence, my love life was rubbish. No sex for three years, if you can believe it. No cashmere jumper purchasing. Mum says I put men off because I'm so successful, because I compete with them in a man's world. And I say, Mum, I mean, really, sod that. I turned forty around the same time, of course, which didn't help.

The day I turned forty I actually heard my waistline go "twang". I was staying at Mum's having my birthday fry-up and there was this twang, and I thought, what's that melancholy sound? Is it a faraway lift-cable snapping? Is it the cat brushing softly against my old guitar in the wardrobe? And then I tried to hold my stomach in and it just wouldn't go, and I thought, of course. Bugger. It's all over. Elasticated waistbands from here on in.

Mum thinks my job must be a marvellous way to meet men. And that's certainly true. I meet thousands. But unfortunately, at the same time, they don't really meet me. Jeff is a good mate – I mean we had the thing in the taxi but it didn't mean anything. He rang me a couple of times afterwards and I said, "Let's be friends" and it's been fine. With the blokes in the office it's all right, too: I'm a sort-of Mother Goose figure, I think. Jeff and I are mummy and daddy. But generally, in the world of football, well – there ought to be scientific studies, actually. Because you know how cats can see only movement? Well, blokes in the world of football have a very similar sort of visual refinement. They can only see women if they've got 22-inch waists and are dancing semi-naked on a table.

It's absolutely true. If a woman of any other description heaves into their field of vision, the eye tells the brain to see a weird unfocused blur, while also, and this is the truly amazing bit, triggering an urgent need to discuss the sexual merits of women they have shagged and women they would like to shag, and what makes a woman shaggable, so as to offend the weird unfocused blur and make it go away. Mum said I should be careful, she read in the paper that taking an interest in football has an effect on your hormones, your testosterone goes up, you start turning into a man. And I thought, well, surely not, I've still got those sticky-out bits that Laurence likes. But on the other hand, if I did start to grow a long grey beard and never put the loo seat down, it might be worth it to start registering on some retinas.

Jeff rang just now. He wanted to remind me there was a documentary about Glenn Hoddle on BBC2. He said if I wanted to talk about it afterwards he'd be up till about one, or even two. I'm beginning to think he hasn't got enough to do with himself, our Jeff.

Scene Three: it's a week later. The football results are on the radio, that famous voice that goes "Heart of Midlothian five" and tells the blokes it's about 5 p.m.

So Laurence finally came round. That's the good news. I was beginning to think I was going to have to bid some sort of symbolic farewell to my sex life – drown my whistle in the fish tank or something. So at least he showed up, which was great. Five to three I put the door on the latch and hopped into bed with the curtains drawn. Radio Five softly in the background. Everything hunky dory. I'd even had a bath. Three o'clock he puts his head round the door and says, "Sue?" and I know just from the way he says it that we're in trouble. "Over here!" I call. Or did I growl it? I think I did. [*Deep sexy voice*] "Over here!" And then I see he's got a suitcase and I shoot out of bed saying, "What's that?" And he says, "Yolanda –" and he sits down on the edge of the bed and starts to cry.

And from then on it was ghastly. I felt trapped. What are you supposed to do when they cry? [*Impatient*] I mean, I know it sounds selfish, but I was looking forward to this afternoon! I'd been looking forward to it for two weeks!

On Radio Five Live, Manchester United versus Newcastle. Cans laid in. Everything perfect. And now Laurence was sitting on the end of my bed snivelling into a tissue, and I thought well, I couldn't help it, I thought honestly, is this supposed to make me fancy you? It was terribly confusing. Something Mum said kept flashing into my mind: "Sue, don't get involved with a married man; you won't be able to stand all the tears and heartache." And it was true. Here I had a married man weeping all over my candlewick and I did not like it at all.

I didn't know what to do. On the radio, Paul Scholes scored with a thirty-yard volley from Beckham, bringing his premiership total to twelve for the season. [*Sing-song*] "Laurence," I said. "Laurence?" He sniffed and wiped his face. [*Sing-song*] "Has something happened?" I really tried to sound caring. "Is it Yolanda? Did she find out?" He nodded, still apparently too overcome with emotion to speak. [*Making light*] "She'll get over it," I said. He looked up at me like a funny old faithful doggie or something. "I told her I was in love with you," he said, quietly. "Oh," I said. I pulled away. "A nice cup of Bovril and we'll sort all this out," I said, and I went to the kitchen and shut the door.

Well, a lot of questions raced through my mind as I made that Bovril, I can tell you. Had I done anything to deserve this? Was the kitchen window big enough to climb out? Could Newcastle pull back before half-time? Was a shag still out of the question? When I went back in, Laurence had taken his clothes off and got into my bed. "I'm OK now," he said. "Can we have a cuddle, please?" I said of course and got in beside him, kissed him on the forehead, smoothed his hair. "That sounded like a great goal from Scholes," I said. He kissed me. He snuggled down and put his head against my shoulder. I could feel my shoulder getting a bit wet, but I didn't say anything. This man in my bed; I wanted him, didn't I? Why wasn't I happy? We lay there and listened, and in the end he fell asleep. Newcastle equalised before half-time, and then Man U got a penalty in the fifty-ninth minute, which Andy Cole drove into the bottom right-hand corner.

Scene Four: the office, background clatter

Jeff's been very odd since he heard about Laurence moving in. Sometimes I think these chestal protuberances of mine have got a lot to answer for. One minute Jeff and I are mates, the next we're all over each other at the Christmas do, then I'm bossing him about and he's loving it; then he's doing a green-eyed Othello – I tell you, I don't know where I am sometimes with blokes. Pickering's just as bad. Sometimes I'm his token woman editor, then I'm one of the lads, then I'm a little delicate flower, then I'm a shoulder to cry on. There's only one thing I won't stand for, and that's when his secretary passes on my grievances, and they miraculously stop being grievances and become "worries". I say, tell Pickering I'm not putting up with this production schedule, and when he comes back he says, "I hear from Janine you're worried about something." I say, "Worried, Janine? Did I say I was worried?" But it's ingrained in him. Pete who edits *Hits-a-Million* is allowed to be angry. John at *Bigguns* is allowed to be furious and snort coke in the lift. Gerry at *Fast and Wheelie* can be incandescent with rage. But Sue can't be angry; she has to be worried. Poor old worryguts Sue just can't sleep at night.

Of course the office found out straight away about my adulterous love-nest when Yolanda came storming in on Monday morning accusing me of stealing her husband. Not a trace of foreign accent, I've no idea where I got that from. She could say "Laurence" with the "L", in fact she said it with the L several times. She also called me a bitch with a B and a whore with a W and she threw a cup of tea over me. Not a natural blonde, I think. Apparently she gave Laurence her child-bearing years, and now wishes she hadn't. She wanted to get a look at me, find out what Laurence saw in me. I said she was welcome, but she should bear in mind I wasn't usually drenched in tea, so make allowances. And then Jeff saw her out and told Ernie in reception not to let her in again if she tried to come back. Apparently as she was leaving she shouted something about complaining to Pickering. So I went straight up to Pickering and told him my side of the story first. I even got one of the Five-a-Side to throw some more tea over me, to enhance my cause. "Don't worry, Sue," he said, as I was leaving. And for once I let it pass.

The thing is, if Laurence went back to Yolanda, I really wouldn't mind. He's not bringing out the best in me. I had a nightmare last night about Bronnley lemons, I was buried under them, suffocating. And he's being such a sap. One night Laurence said, "I'm so happy." [*Sigh*] And I snapped, "It'll pass." He's been writing stuff every day, which makes it worse. I'm not his wife! But he reads me bits in the evening about incredibly old South American women who suddenly lift donkeys in the air or give birth to iguanas while parrots form feathery rainbows above their heads. I mean, [*really impatient*] what's all that about? I'm scared to go home. I go to the pub after work each night with the Five-a-Side. He phones me at the office and I don't phone him back.

Scene Five: Saturday afternoon footie on radio, abruptly switched off, with "Oh shut up"

Well, there's good news and bad news. Laurence left on Wednesday – that's the good news. He went back to Yolanda, leaving me a letter saying he would always love me, he'd never met anyone like me, tear-stained, you know. And then Pickering called me in on Thursday and sacked me. There had been a tiny piece in a paper on Monday about Laurence falling prey to a vampish and busty hackette, and that was enough. "The man is unbalanced," I objected. "He thinks having casual sex means being in love. That's not reasonable, is it?" But sexual harassment is what Pickering called it, and seemed positively ecstatic to point out sexual harassment applied as much to women as to men. He started saying, "What's goose for the gander" and then stopped because he couldn't remember it. "Laurence doesn't actually work for me," I pointed out. "Ah, but he's not the only person who's complained," Pickering said. He said I should take the money, go home, and in a couple of weeks he'd see if I wanted a less high-profile job on another title, possibly taking over the ailing magazine they set up in competition to *Gardening Which* – which they called *Gardening What*. I was dumbstruck. [*Incredulous*] They wanted me to save a magazine called *Gardening What*?

It was too much to take in. Especially when I got back to the office and found Jeff ensconced. Of course. The complainant. The snog. "Pickering has asked me to take over," he said. "It's much better for the magazine this way, Sue." He emptied some feminine toiletries out of my office drawer, with the look of someone who's never seen anything like them before. He probably thought Tampax was the name of a side in the Greek second division. He didn't admit he'd been plotting my downfall. All he said, rather sadly, was, "You used to be really nice."

[*Radio switched on for the football results*] So here I am. I just kept thinking, "How would this look if it were the other way round?" But I can't sort that out, it's too confusing, I just feel sort of double-crossed. There ought to be a book called *Men Who Want Women to be Men, and the Women Who Go Along with It*. I'll write it if no one else will. Men do want women to be like them, you know. It's not just Professor Higgins. And I've worked out why. Men want women to be more like men because then they don't have to feel guilty about dumping on us. And then, the gits, they dump on us anyway.

[*Results in background*] I had a little cry last night about Laurence. But how could I let him say he loved me? [*Distracted*] Blimey, five-nil, that's a turn-up. In the old days when a Bronnley lemon was a romantic highlight, it would have been nice to think I was loved. But as I said to Mum last night, I'm sorry, I've reached a certain age and I just can't be vulnerable to blokes any more. I know how their minds work, Mum. I know too much about them.

[*Recovers*] *Gardening What*, I ask you. *Gardening Why* more like it. I'll tell you what though. Mendelssohn got stretchered off on his first appearance this afternoon. [*Laughs*] His left foot was superlative, apparently; even his left leg was special. The fans were thrilled, fifteen million well spent. But after a quarter of an hour he collided with his own keeper, and his right leg broke in three places.

Like pistol shots apparently. Crack, crack, crack. Fifteen minutes they got out of him; a million quid a minute. I'm wondering if I might ring Chris Eubank later. I know his number, after all.

The Pedant

*ALASTAIR works in a rare book shop in central London;
he is generally in despair at the stupidity of other people,
and does not disguise this very well. He's not posh; in fact,
a lot of his attitude comes from the fact that he is largely
self-educated. His small flat in Covent Garden is rent-
controlled and full of books. He hasn't had a girlfriend
for many years. When he quotes other people, he has a
tendency to give them a stupid voice.*

*Scene One: central London café with low hubbub; it is around
9.30 in the morning on a rainy, wintry day; Alastair is listening
to conversation at a nearby table, but we can't hear it; he talks
in a kind of angry whisper, with harrumphs*

Why don't they hang up signs in public places? "Please
desist from doing easy crosswords out loud if you are
phenomenally stupid." This was supposed to be MY ten

minutes: MY ten minutes when I have a double espresso – which they do quite well here, although I told them last time quite clearly, biscotti being a plural form in the first place, there can obviously be no such word as "biscotties". Anyway, this is supposed to be my ten minutes, in which I peruse this stunning 1895 vellum edition of Ovid's *Metamorphoses* – the one with the Beardsley linocuts – before swooping down on the biannual Chelsea Book Fair in search of similar leather-bound treasures for Nick's shop. But can I concentrate? No. Why? Because of some idiots, equipped with a copy of the *Daily Idiot*, trying to fill in the more idiotic of the idiots' crosswords. "Bee-oh-wolf," she said just now. And I'm supposed to sit here, studying an illustration of Philomel being turned into a nightingale, and not interfere? "Bee-oh-wolf, four letters, second letter P," she says. [*Stupid sing-song clueless noise*] "Oh," says her clueless friend. I haven't seen either of them properly, but the second one sounded remarkably like that woman Nick set me up with for his fortieth birthday – which he did, as usual, without conducting even the most basic compatibility research. "What's a Bee-oh-wolf then?" "Dunno," says the first one, "I don't think there ARE any four-letter words with P as the second letter, are there? Perhaps your "Nipple" is wrong –" and I think I can't stand this, so I call across, [*snappy*] "Epic, the answer's epic, you stupid woman!" and then go back to my book. Of course, that was only the beginning. "Who said that?" "He did. Bloke with the beard." "What's it got to do with him?"

[*Pause; hubbub; he stirs coffee and sips it*] I'm trying not to listen, but ... [*sigh*]. I made a policy decision some years ago, you see, that in this sort of situation, I just won't suffer in silence. And sometimes it does prevent more agony, because, all right, they may laugh at me and call me names, but I manage, on occasion, to [*raises voice a bit, to be heard*] SHAME THEM INTO SILENCE.

[*Short pause; the hubbub is continuous; he picks up something new. Impatient*] Not these two, though; it's unbelievable, unbelievable; they're still at it. [*He blurts out another answer*] Waterfall! The answer's waterfall! Cataract! Nine letters beginning with W! Water, five letters. Fall, four letters. Meaning: a cataract. It's no good, I can't stand this. It's torture. [*Calls out*] It's all right, madam, I'm going.

[*He gathers his things hurriedly, swigs his coffee*] I'm going, you win, welcome to the Kingdom of Barbaria! I'm going, I'm going, the field is yours.

Scene Two: evening: Alastair is at home; classical music in background. He is quite tired and oddly happy; having a hot drink at bedtime

[*He drinks*] Ah. Cocoa. Those Aztecs knew a thing or two. Yes, after a day of hard, gruelling human sacrifice and baking poor little guinea pigs inside lumps of mud, curl up with a nice cup of cocoa. [*Drinks*] *Life Groomers*, I'd never even heard of it; apparently it gets an audience of two million, but then, let's face it, so would hanging, drawing and quartering if they brought it back, so that's hardly a watertight argument for taking part in it. I still don't quite believe the way today turned out. I mean, it started typically enough, with those Thicky Sisters at that café cudgelling their atom-sized brains over simple synonyms. [*Sips happily*] The Fair went well, I returned to Nick's shop at 3 p.m. with my antiquarian treasures, which had been hilariously under-priced by Thatched Cottage Books of Alfriston, and we had a cup of Lapsang to celebrate, and Nick complained about the customers, who were (as usual) within earshot, while I re-shelved the fiction, having noticed that M. R. James had got alphabetically the wrong side of Henry James, which is typical of the sort of morons you get browsing in Charing Cross Road bookshops these days, and I was just back to leafing through *Metamorphoses* when Nick coughed and mentioned in a rather uncomfortable way that, ahem, well, the thing was, a couple of people were coming in this afternoon to see me. Of course, at this point, I was still blissfully innocent of what was about to unfold. "To see ME?" I said. "Why?" For one wild moment, I wondered if I was winning a pub quiz trophy – for my years of dedication or outstanding brilliance. But it wasn't that. He looked at the clock, gulped, and said in a rush, [*quite anxious*] "Alastair, I hope you won't mind, but I put you forward for *Life Groomers*." I said, "Oh." Well, I didn't know what *Life Groomers* was, so I waited for a bit more information. He said, look, it's been a long time since Geraldine, hasn't it? And I said yes, ha, twelve years, why d'you ask? Well, he said, I'm going to tell you straight here, Alastair, as a friend. [*Hard to say it to best friend*] You're not attractive to women.

WHAT? I said. I mean, [*hollow laugh*] I'm sorry, but this is NICK! "Alastair," he says, "you're a nice person. You have a lot of love to give. These Life Groomer people will give you techniques to make you come over AS a nice person instead of – instead of as [*this still stings*] a lonely pedantic short-tempered beardy-weirdy. Change is a good thing. I mean, that book you're reading. That's all about change, isn't it?"

So I was just saying, "Yes, Nick, but the people in this book are mostly turned, against their will, into TREES" when half a dozen people came in, just like that, door opens, bell goes ding-a-ling-a-ling, man with a camera with a light on top of it, Nick says, "Oops, they're here," and in they march. [*It's an awful memory*] I stand there blinking like the proverbial rabbit in the headlights. "You must be Alastair!" says this man with a comical haircut and thick orange make-up. "Good man! I'm Jake from *Life Groomers*. Great stuff. Meet the team! Great stuff! Jancis ("Hello!") is going to help you with haircut, wardrobe and, er, strategic shaving; Baxter ("Hi, man!") will improve that oh-so negative body language of yours; and Phoebe ("Lovely to meet you!") will attempt to train you out of certain linguistic habits. We've been filming you secretly for a couple of weeks already. Are you surprised?" [*Pause, stunned*] "Yes, I am surprised." "Good man! The girl with the very thick glasses is the production assistant Shakira ([*a whisper*] "Hello"), she's a bit shy, and that's Chazza with the clipboard ([*idiot voice*] "Hi, man"), anything at all you want to know, ask Chazza." He paused for me to say something about how thrilled I was. I didn't. I merely wondered, since Jake had said I could ask Chazza anything at all, what would happen if I asked him the capital of Botswana. "Great stuff. Excellent. What more can I say? Welcome to *Life Groomers*!" At which point, everyone in the shop, including a couple of my least favourite customers who were loitering in the travel section, burst into wild applause.

[*Drinks*] The only good thing about the whole experience was seeing Nick's expression. He looked like he'd just watched his best friend and long-time employee run over by a tank. Which, in a way, he had. I let him stew. I wasn't so much angry with him as shocked. When Jake and most of the others had gone, leaving Chazza and Shakira behind to explain the formalities, I went and stood in the back yard, in the drizzling rain, and I was actually shaking. Before they left, the Life Groomers had given me some bits of instant advice, by way of a free sample. And these helpful hints were: stop hunching; lose the floppy bow-tie; and stop passing hurtful snap judgements on other people's inferior intellectual capacity.

[*Drinks*] Morons. I came back inside.

[*Serious*] "Do you have any misgivings, Alastair?" said Shakira. Her glasses were so thick, I noticed, that her eyes behind them looked quite tiny. She was frowning and serious.

"You might say that," I said. "Look, the way I see it is this. If I come across as a lonely, pedantic beardy-weirdy" – I looked at Nick when I said this, in the hope that he would have the grace to look embarrassed, instead of which he prompted, "Don't forget short-tempered". "All right," I said. "If I come across LIKE THAT, isn't it just possible that a lonely, pedantic, short-tempered beardy-weirdy is what I am?"

Shakira folded her arms and for a few moments looked at them in silence. Chazza – concentrating on his clipboard – started drawing pictures of windmills to pass the time. At last, she spoke. "Do you know Michelangelo's unfinished sculpture in Florence?"

[*Impressed, but suspicious*] "Er, yes," I said. She had a sweet little face behind those glasses.

"Well," said Shakira, "to me, you see, that figure, the way it's half-emerged from the block of marble, sort of struggling to be born – I think that answers your doubts about *Life Groomers*."

"Er, in what way?"

"Some of us don't want to be helped out of our blocks of marble, even though we sense we are only half-finished. But if we are released, with expert help, we are still the same material, you see. [*She's warming up*] I mean, the statue is still marble. Which shows that it's possible to change yet remain the same. I promise you, Alastair, you will ALWAYS be essentially a pedantic beardy-weirdy. You just may not always be a lonely one."

Nick gave me a look, as if to say, "You see?" I gave him a returning look that said, "Oh bog off, you Judas."

She had another thought. [*Light*] "Chazza, do you remember Jeremy?"

[*Puzzled*] "That geezer who'd never had a girlfriend?"

"Jeremy's problem was that he was like the unfinished statue."

Chazza snorted. "Yeah. But he also had a gigantic conk."

Scene Three: the date. The bathroom of a restaurant, where Alastair is being filmed on a date; he is agitated. Sounds of loos flushing, taps, hand-driers, etc. When he impersonates Caroline, she's quite posh-sounding

I am trying. But I think this may be the worst torture ever devised by the mind of man. "Just have to go to the Gents," I said – and I could tell she was a bit puzzled; after all, this is the third time I've come in here, and we're only halfway through the soup. I just keep thinking, look, I'm in here trying to be pleasant to a complete stranger in an extraordinarily provocative frock, and outside in a surveillance caravan there's Jancis, Baxter and Phoebe, all making [*exaggerated "that's interesting" sound*] "O-o-oh" noises, and ticking a box every time I say the word "stupid".

A shame they wouldn't let me do this dummy-run with Shakira. I did ask. If it was Shakira, you see, I wouldn't have to pretend to be interested in her. [*Knows it sounds mean*] Oh, look, I didn't mean that the way it sounded. It's just that before she left the shop the other day, she bought a book about early French cinema, and when I said, "There's a complete Jean Vigo DVD out now," and she said, "I know, I've ordered it," it was just like, you know, chatting. If it weren't for the chronic myopia and the crippling shyness, she'd be all right. It turned out she'd even booked to see some of that Jean Cocteau season at the NFT, featuring that rarely seen extra footage from *La Belle et la Bête*.

However, the Life Groomers just laughed when I suggested Shakira for the date, and instead I've got this agonising bore called Caroline, and I've been trying SO HARD to take an interest in everything about her: her job, her ex-husband, her friend's ex-husband's catastrophic skiing accident (actually, that was quite interesting), and her ex-husband's friend's daughter's cat. They said to me the other day, "All you know is facts, Alastair. Most people like to talk about THEMSELVES." But, God, it's tiring when you have to fill in the pauses. "Tell me about that, Caroline; oh but WHY did you do that; how did you FEEL when you did that?" And then I have to pinch myself, literally, at the top of the thigh, otherwise I'll slip into a coma. Even her solecisms are dull – "disinterested" for "uninterested" [*sigh*], although [*perversely impressed*] I don't think I've ever heard anyone say "aircrafts" before. I don't dare correct her. The Life Groomers will be alarmed enough already, I reckon, what with me nervously drinking pints of water, and reaching compulsively under the table to interfere with my own leg.

[*Loo flushing or other bathroom noise*]

Scene Four: at home

It was only when I was signing the release form that I realised the problem. We were in the production office, it was quite intimidating, brightly lit, hundreds of computer terminals, dozens of under-25s in fashionable specs, wearing tech-y earpieces and important, faraway expressions. But, strangely, I felt quite welcome. And when we watched the tape to see how scary I was to Caroline – who characterised me afterwards as "hairy and weirdly aggressive, like an angry hobbit" – I knew I couldn't go back. I couldn't go back, because I'd already started. They were all delighted, thrilled, and so on – not least because, with me on board, they now had a full series, the plan being to slot me between a woman with self-esteem issues and a bloke who stinks, a pair affectionately nicknamed "The Cringer" and "The Whiffer". But there was one problem. They want to groom me in May, culminating on Sunday the 17th, which happens to be the date of the London Pub Quiz Championship final in Highbury. "Sorry, Alastair," said Baxter, "but can't your saddo quiz mates manage without you?" – which is the most insensitive thing any of them has ever said to me, and you should hear Jancis on the subject of my cardigans.

Then Jake had an idea. "Look," he said. "I've got it. Shakira takes Alastair's place in the quiz team. Problem solved. Great stuff."

Shakira looked a bit panicky. Her glasses steamed up. She bit her lip.

"Oh come on, Shakira!" he said. "You've got this IQ of – what is it? A hundred or something?"

"A hundred and eighty-five," she said.

Jake looked at me. "What do you say to that?" he said.

[*Alastair can't get over it*] "A hundred and EIGHTY-FIVE?"

[*As Shakira*] "But I've never done a pub quiz."

"Quick, Alastair, ask her a question."

"Oh. Right. Um, Shakira, which London Underground station shares its name with a station on the Paris Métro?"

"Er ... [*works it out, quickly; with assurance*] Temple!" she said.

They all looked clueless.

"Is that good?" Jake said.

"Oh yes," I said. "That's very good."

"Well, that's solved that, then," said Jake. "Well done. Great stuff. Good man. Top job."

I signed the form. I'd done enough shilly-shallying. And something was happening to me, I knew that. I didn't just want to know facts any more. When Shakira said "Temple", she suddenly had this special look, you see, the look known to quizzers as "the flash" – it's the look of pure joy you get when you just KNOW. And I felt pleased for her, because it marked her out as "one of us", but sort of melancholy for myself, because that flash is the only happiness I know, and it comes from being one hundred per cent certain how to spell the word "minuscule". While we're on the subject, though, Nick frequently has the flash with questions about motor racing, and the thing is, motor racing doesn't interest him and it NEVER HAS. Spooky, eh? "Emerson Fittipaldi!" he says; "Ayrton Senna!" We think Nick may have a direct psychic connection to Murray Walker's brain. We don't know how it came about. But it's tremendously convenient, none the less.

Scene Five: a pub. It's a few weeks later; Alastair is waiting for Nick

Nick should be along in a minute. I'm not going to put up with any more of his nonsense about these fancy specs. ALL this is his fault, from the tip of the trendy haircut to the soles of the shiny shoes. Even the proceedings of last night can be laid at his door, come to think of it. [*Drinks*] Which makes me feel slightly better about it. Oh, they were so pleased with me on *Life Groomers*, you see. Right up until last night. Four weeks of slog, and they were saying mine might be the best personality make-over ever. I went for hours at a stretch without calling anybody stupid. I was a success story. I was going to be great TV.

And now I've blown it. Oh, where's Nick got to? Yesterday, you see, was the night of my last filmed date, and also the final of the pub quiz. Shakira and I met beforehand at the office, to wish each other luck. Over the past four weeks I've seen a lot of her, obviously, as she's trained for the big night; I've become quite proud of her, to be honest. We both, separately, went to see *La Belle et la Bête*, and interestingly we both preferred it WITHOUT the extra footage. We both thought Cocteau had been right not to labour that crucial transfiguration scene. Meanwhile the quiz team – Nick, plus Trensher and Hoppy – all welcomed her on board, and I enjoyed watching a natural quizzer really come out of herself. So last night when we met to say, "Good luck, Alastair," – "Good luck, Shakira," it was a bit unsettling when she suddenly fixed me with this meaningful look and said, [*very serious, very upset*] "Oh, Alastair!" and ran off in the general direction of Highbury.

I was confused, to say the least. What was all that about? Then Chazza came over with a cup of tea. He's an idiot, Chazza, although obviously these days I try to avoid the "I" word, but I've grown to like him. I thought how amazing it was that a month ago I'd never even met these people: now they appeared to be my whole life.

"Big night, Al, yeah?" said Chazza.

"Yeah," I said.

"What gel you using?"

"Couldn't say, mate."

"Scared?"

"Not really."

"Huh," he said. [*Between you and me*] "Hope you do better than the Whiffer, eh!"

I laughed. I'd heard on the grapevine that the Whiffer's muscular BO had effortlessly triumphed over all attempts to quell it. On his final date, the woman had edged further and further away from him until her chairleg went off the edge of the platform they were sitting on, and she'd somersaulted backwards down some stairs.

"Chazza," I said.

"Yeah?"

"All these weeks I've kept meaning to ask. There's the Cringer and the Whiffer. What does that make ME?"

[*Cheerfully*] "Oh, you're the Pedant."

Ah. Well, it could have been worse. But I was crushed

anyway. I didn't tell him I'd secretly been hoping for "the Loner".

"Chazza," I said again.

"Yeah?"

"Is there anything wrong with Shakira?"

"Why?"

"She seemed a bit odd when she went off tonight."

[*Confidential*] "Oh, she's CHANGED," he said. "She's been a bit funny for weeks, but this afternoon, she suddenly went all peculiar and announced she was leaving. Leaving immediately. Said she couldn't work any more on a show that glorified manufactured external attractiveness."

"Really? That's a shame. Oh, that's such a shame."

"We think it came home to her that she's a bit, you know, a bit of a dog, when she heard that conversation between you and Jake."

[*No idea what this is*] "Which conversation?"

"The one when you said she'd be great to take out on a date coz you wouldn't have to take an interest in her."

"Did I say that? I didn't say that!"

[*He thinks about it*] I pictured Shakira's little face, looking up at me, all crumpled, saying, "Oh, Alastair!"

[*Dead*] "I did say that, didn't I?"

"Yeah. We got it on tape if you wanna see it."

I felt terrible. Shakira had been so good to me.

"And Shakira's seen this, has she?"

"Yeah. We had it on in the office just today."

[*Pause. Alarm*] "I didn't say she was a bit of a dog?"

"No, no. Course not. Jake did."

[*Phew*]

"But you didn't say she wasn't."

From then on, funnily enough, I wasn't on very good form.

"This is Gillian."

[*A grunt*]

"Say hello, Alastair."

[*Distant*] "Oh, hello."

It was as if someone had struck me a glancing blow on the head with the back of a shovel. I couldn't snap out of it. Luckily, the Life Groomers had never seen suicidal remorse before, so they assumed I was merely nervous.

"Big night, Alastair!"

[*In agony*] "Mm."

"Good luck!"

[*Sick with guilt*] "Mm!"

All I could think of was Shakira. I was jangled, in torment. As I sat at the table with the lovely Gillian, all I wanted to do was moan aloud with my head in my hands. As a fun date, I ranked just about equal with the ghost in *Hamlet*. How could I have said something so horrible about Shakira? It was unbearable to think about. I only meant that we had a lot in common! I only meant, actually, that she wasn't a tiresome, illiterate egomaniac like all these other women with their sparkly make-up and strappy shoes. Blimey, [*a laugh*] if anything, Shakira and I were made for each other! The other day, as we were walking past a café, she said, "Look, Alastair, fancy writing 'paninis', when panini is ALREADY A PLURAL WORD"!

"Excuse me," I said, "Won't be a sec –" and I ran to the Gents with my mobile, where I tried to phone Nick, but of course all the contestants have their mobiles confiscated and switched off during an all-London final, so there was nothing I could do, nothing. I looked around in a kind of panic. I'd left my wallet in my jacket. If I stayed away from my date for more than a minute, a bunch of well-meaning youths with space-age earpieces would descend on me and ask what was happening. What could I do? I had to speak to Shakira!

There was nothing I could do, I thought, nothing; or nothing unless [*ho ho, not very likely*] I removed my microphone, ran some water to cover any tell-tale noises, climbed out of that toilet window, and sprinted in the rain up to Highbury like something from a Richard Curtis film. [*Beat; he did it*] Blimey, Al, I thought, as I unpinned the mike and reached for the tap. It wasn't in a direction anyone was expecting, but you really have CHANGED.

Scene Six: a few months later, at the café of the first scene; hubbub

Excuse me. [*Raises voice*] Excuse me, the answer you require is "Rayon". "Shedding light on synthetic fabric." "RAY, ON – rayon." That's OK, no problem. [*Smiling, used to having people recognise him; under breath*] Yes, I WAS on the telly. Yes. Yes, I was the ugly, hairy git who was the biggest ever failure on *Life Groomers*. Yes, yes, completely useless. The one who'll never have a girlfriend. Yes, that's me. [*Giving an ironic wave*] Hello!

[*Yet he seems happy. Is this because he has reverted to type? Or did he climb out of that window? We don't yet know*]

We lost that final, you know. It was all Nick's fault, though – not mine, although it may have been a bit distracting for everybody when I burst in at the start of the second round, shouting, [*gasping, exhausted*] "Shakira, I love you! I've been an idiot!" and collapsed from exhaustion and hypothermia on a pile of wet smelly coats in the corner. No, it was Nick. In the last round, they were neck-and-neck with the Hackney bunch when one of those motor racing questions came up and Nick said, [*with great assurance*] "Brands Hatch!" and for the first time ever, it wasn't. Poor old Nick. Murray Walker must have put up a firewall. You can't blame him, really.

But the bursting-in thing was definitely the right thing to do. Because it's been *Life Groomers* in reverse for the past couple of months, and it's been fantastic. Shakira and I take turns pointing out hilarious mistakes on menus. We go and see old French films together on purpose (instead of accidentally) and wait till the very, very end of the credits, drinking in as much information as we can. I've grown back the beard and bought several new cardigans to replace the ones ceremonially shredded by Jancis. Shakira's coming with me this morning to the Chelsea Book Fair, where she'll meet more short-tempered beardy-weirdy book dealers than you can shake a stick at.

"Did you know they called me the Pedant?" I said to Nick yesterday, as we leaned on the counter and stared out mournfully at the cretins on Charing Cross Road.

"Ah," he said.

"Ah?"

"Well, that was me," he said. "When I first contacted them, and I spoke to Shakira about you, she asked if I could come up with a snappy one-word description."

[*Shocked, disappointed*] "And you said Pedant?"

"No, actually, I said 'Tosser' but we decided to tone it down."

"I see," I said. "You don't think 'Loner' would have had more of a ring to it?"

[*Scoff*] "Loner!"

"All right. Calm down."

[*Guffaw*] "Loner!!"

"All right. All right. How about some Lapsang?

Shakira's introduced me to this new one, that's the same but different, if you know what I mean."

[*Mocking*] "The same but different. Like a half-formed statue by Michelangelo? Like the lovely Alastair after *Life Groomers*? Oh Alastair, I've been meaning to say: you do know you've written 'BOOKS' with an apostrophe over there?"

[*Alarmed*] "What? Where? Quick!"

"Ha!" said Nick. "Got you."

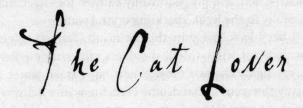

The Cat Lover

*JO is in bed, with the cat. She has been in bed with the cat
for quite some time – i.e. days rather than hours. She is
happy.*

*Scene One: Radio Four – in particular "Woman's Hour" – in
background*

I'm going out mountain-biking again today. [*Happy relaxed
sigh*] After which it's the tennis lesson with Pierre and
a date in the evening with Ron Weasley, the jet-setting
Californian dotcom millionaire I met on my first day.
Currently, however – hang on, I can't concentrate with
Jenni Murray talking about incontinence pads – [*switches
off radio*] currently, however, as you can see, I am floating
on my back in the turquoise hotel pool in my day-glow
orange swimsuit, relaxing after a vigorous sea-salt scrub
executed by a Swedish woman in a white coat, the sun

171

kissing my exquisite golden exfoliated body, arms outstretched, and my beautifully painted toes stretching blissfully in the light, sparkling crystal water.

I bet I look lovely in this swimsuit. Tanned thighs, narrow waist, wide athletic shoulders, glittering jewellery. [*Happy sigh; eats toast through next bit*] I tread water to survey the scene. A handsome Frenchie waiter delivers a cool fruit punch to my sun lounger, where my third fat romantic novel of the week so far – packed with episodes of hot sex at polo tournaments amongst the internationally rich and famous – crisps and curls under the fierce rays of the Mediterranean sun. There are clinking and bustling sounds from the kitchens, where a buffet lunch of tasty haute cuisine low-cal savouries and oily salads is taking shape. The odd female scream from the nearby beach. [*Jerked back to reality*] Where's the cat gone? Buster? [*Indulgent*] Oh there you are. [*Back to scene*] Where was I? Oh yes. And here's Ron Weasley back from shopping in St Tropez, diving neatly into the pool to splash water at me and make me laugh my tinkly laugh. [*Suddenly serious*] I wish I hadn't chosen the name Ron Weasley. But that's the trouble with getting the names out of your *Harry Potter* in a bit of a panic when your friend Linda phones out of the blue and asks how you're getting on. However, look on the bright side. At least I didn't choose Hagrid. At least I didn't choose Voldemort.

I don't feel a bit guilty about deceiving Linda. The thing is, she would never have let me spend my week's holiday in bed with the cat. I know that sounds ridiculous – your friends can't control your life, can they, however opinionated and bossy they may be. But with Linda, I don't know how it happened, I'm ten years older than her for a start, but sorting me out seems to have become her life's work, and I don't have much of a say in it. Perhaps you've never got into this situation with a friend, where in terms of bowing to superior knowledge she's the big white missionary with the bible and you're the native with the blow pipe and the bone through his nose. But that's how it is with me and Linda. "Tell you what you should do, Jo," she says. "Get your hair cut. I know what you should do, Jo. Join my gym; there's a discount at the moment, you could come with me at lunchtimes. Here's what I've decided, Jo. Get rid of the cat." Bought Ledger used to be such a happy department. But since Linda came six months ago, she's appointed herself my older sister, confessor, guru, unpaid personal trainer and saviour of my soul. You know that programme *Would Like to Meet* on the TV? Where an expert panel of smug midgets with bright lipstick interfere with some poor woman to make her more desirable to the opposite sex? Well, imagine those smug midgets rolled into one nightmare colleague sitting at the next desk in Bought Ledger and, trust me, that's Linda.

She was the one who insisted I go on holiday to the South of France. "You're turning into a cat lady, Jo" – that's what she said. A cat lady? Well thanks a lot. "You've got to clear that picture of Buster off your desk, Jo. You've got to stop reading books called things like *Moggy and Me*. Just because Jeff was a louse who messed up your flat and took some of your belongings, you've given up on men and you sit watching *Would Like to Meet* shouting bitter ripostes like, 'Why don't you look at yourselves for a change!' with the cat resting its paws round your neck. I'm coming with you to book that holiday at once." So we went to the travel agents and before I knew what was happening, I'd booked a very expensive seven-night package on the Côte d'Azur. Linda spent the next week picking swimwear out of a catalogue. Of course I went back to cancel the holiday the same afternoon, which really hacked off the girl with the short skirt and the grubby keyboard, but there you are. I know I should have told Linda what I'd done. But seeing her so happy, you see – seeing her live each day to the full like that – it seemed a kindness not to tell her.

Which was why, when I left work last Friday saying, "See you soon! Thanks for all the factor eight!" I felt she had left me with no choice as to how I spent the following week. I got home, locked the door, unplugged the phone and just went to bed with the cat, where I have now been lying and luxuriating without significant interruption for [*excited*] four whole days (!). [*Happy sigh, yawn*] Sometimes I turn this way [*turns over, rustle of bed linen*] and sometimes I turn that way [*more rustling*]. The only fly in the ointment is that every day at 2 p.m., I have to put down my *Harry Potter* and answer my mobile. Because it's Linda, you see. Checking up on my progress, on her way back to work from the gym. "Hello!" I yell, as if I'm answering at some exotic distance and not actually just half a mile away from Worrington's in my flat in South Croydon. "Linda? Sorry, can't talk! Too busy with swimming pool, French blokes, exercise, Swedish massage, that sort of thing!" And then I switch off the phone for another day and give Buster a fantastic comprehensive stroke which starts with the gorgeous pussycat back-of-the-head bit between his ears, travels along all the ridges of his beautiful tabby back and ends with an affectionate yank of his lovely, lovely tail.

I'd have switched the mobile off completely if I hadn't found this. [*Cuckoo clock noise*] Hang on. That's track 6.

Track 5. Here we are. [*Beach sound; waves; distant laughter*]
It's a BBC sound effects record Jeff rather typically left
inside my Shania Twain CD case. I discovered it quite
quickly, because obviously when we split up just before
Christmas it was Gutsy Shania I turned to. But what did
I find when I put her on? Was it a glamorous country
gal with ballsy attitude in a floorlength leopardskin coat
and hood singing, "That don't impress me much"? No,
it was a lark ascending. "What?" I said. "Tweet, tweet-
tweet, tweet, tweet," it went. "Twit-twit." Well, I thought,
as I took it out of the machine, [*Shania quote*] THAT don't
impress me much. But then I recognised the hand of
Jeff, of course, and I had a little weep. You always got
something back from Jeff, you see – however insultingly
small and randomly chosen. Give him a car, and by way
of thanks he'd present you with an only slightly soiled
fashion magazine he'd thoughtfully picked up on the
tube. Give him a camera and he'd reciprocate with an
interesting doormat he'd found in a skip. People say cats
bring home presents you don't want, but they should
try living with Jeff. He used to buy CDs for people at
Christmas and tape them first, which I suppose other
people sometimes do without admitting it – but when
Jeff did it there was this tiny difference: he kept the CD
for himself and gave the tape as the present. I remember
he said I was very shallow and ungrateful when I said,
"Hang on, is this what I think it is?" looking at a tape
with "Van Morrison" scribbled on it. He said nobody had
minded before. But I looked at my tape and said I bet
they have, actually, and he said that any views on normal
human relations coming from a person who idolised a
pussy cat should be treated with extreme caution, and
I said, oh bog off and die, Jeff, which I seem to think he

shortly afterwards actually did, except for the dying part as far as I know.

Anyway, the rough inventory I made after he left showed he'd taken not only my Shania Twain, but an enormous number of biros, half the bedding, all the storage jars, the fridge, and what was the other thing? Oh yes, I nearly forgot, my childbearing years. In return for which, at first I couldn't find anything at all, and was quite wounded, until I found this sound effects sampler CD which certainly wasn't mine, and probably wasn't Jeff's originally either – somebody else had probably chucked it out and Jeff had snapped it up as always, doubtless thinking – as he always did about broken chairs or quarter-full paint tins – that it was just far too precious to be thrown away.

[*Sound of lark ascending*] This bit's lovely, though. I'd love to know exactly what sort of bird it is, but of course typically I don't have the list. But as I say, it's been a godsend. The first day Linda rang, I picked up the mobile in alarm, and was just about to switch it off when I thought hang on, selected a track at random, and found this [*airport noises*]. It was a miracle. I was saved. "I'm at the airport, Linda!" I yelled. "Feeling immensely energised! You were right about me needing to get away! Thanks, Linda, speak to you soon, they're calling my flight!" and hung up in case the track finished abruptly. The next day, when she rang again at the same time, I skipped through the tracks and found this [*restaurant hubbub noises, quite loud*]. Fantastic. "Who?" I shouted. "Linda? Linda, sorry, can't talk. Yes! Fantastic time! Met a chap called" – hasty perusal of *Harry Potter and the Goblet of Fire* – "Ron Weasley! You were so right!" At which point I turned it up. [*More hubbub, turned up*] 'Oui, pour moi le salade niçoise, merci!

Avec les haricots françaises!' Sorry, Linda, speak to you soon." Then I hung up, turned off the CD, put the radio back on for *The Archers* and lay flat on the bed till Buster climbed on my chest for a snoozing session that lasted the full distance of *The Afternoon Play* and right through to *PM* at five.

Scene Two: still in bed. Soft classical music in background

I first got Buster when he was six weeks old. That was fifteen years ago. He'd been called Fizzy by the children who owned his mother, but because he was a rather small and feeble newborn tabby-and-white kitten when I first saw him – the only one of the four-day-old litter unable to climb out a low-sided box – I challenged this tiny animal, "Come on, Buster, put 'em up" and although I considered some other names during his weaning period, it was Buster that stuck. Once it has dawned on you that calling a kitten Buster makes him, well, Buster Kitten, the idea becomes irresistible. Had he been a girl-cat, I always say, I would have called him Diane. Anyway, it turned out to suit my cat to be named after Old Stoneface Himself, because truly he's a comparable master of body language. When there's anyone else in the flat, such as Jeff, Buster can just sit with his back to them and sort of hunch his shoulders in a way that speaks more contempt and hostility than mere words could ever express. I worked out Buster's horoscope once, and I won't go into his moon in Virgo or his lucky number or anything, because you'll think I'm incredibly sad, but he's a Cancer cat, which makes him especially territorial. Bless him. He was also born in the Chinese year of the Tiger – which is handy, as it must be very confusing for cats to be born in the year of the Dog, mustn't it? Or dogs to be born in the year of the Snake, or indeed rats in the year of the Aardvark or whatever it is. In fact, you'd think the Chinese would have thought of that really. It casts doubt on the whole system when you look at it that way.

Anyway, the point is, Cancer Tiger or whatever he is, I don't seem to be able to judge Buster. I just love him. Unconditionally. Forgive him anything. Pat him on the bonce whatever he's done and say, "Who's my darling boy, then?" No wonder it drove Jeff bananas. As he often pointed out, if BUSTER had made me a tape of Van Morrison I'd be – well, surprised, obviously, but also thrilled to the core. Meanwhile, I am also incredibly entertained by Buster. Say I get a man in to service the boiler. Buster strolls in, sighs, shoots me an accusing glare and then climbs on the man's toolbox, and won't get off. And it cracks me up. That's my boy. When new friends innocently say, "Is he a friendly cat?", Buster takes one look at them and goes to his litter box and starts making unmistakeably hostile pawing-through-gravel noises inside it, and what do I do? I shrug with an indulgent smile. I say, [*lightly*] "He always does this!" I must seem like one of those terrible mothers of infant delinquents who say, "Well, you shouldn't leave it lying about, should you?" and offer to duff up the teachers at the school.

Rather touchingly, Jeff started off pretending to be fond of Buster. I remember they watched snooker together at the start, and that Jeff found it quite amusing when Buster stood up on his hind legs in front of the telly and tried to pat the balls as they travelled across the screen. Then the male bonding started to come slightly unglued, then peeled apart as fondness cooled and there was a period of each tolerating the other when Jeff didn't watch the snooker any more, and even on one memorable occasion (rather childishly, I thought) mocked Buster's efforts to operate the remote. In the end, of course, it descended to naked aggression, and when one day Jeff left the front door open "accidentally", and Buster ran across our busy main road and got lost for a day and I roamed the neighbourhood shaking a packet of Kitbits and snivelling and weeping, I said Jeff had better go now and take his fridge with him, along with the storage jars and all the other stuff I may have mentioned including my Shania Twain and hopes of future connubial happiness. Losing Buster had been extremely traumatic. I went along the street checking in bins; I was convinced I would find him dead; I asked old ladies if they'd seen him and they said, "I hope you find him quickly, dear, there's a gang working round here that rounds up lost cats and turns them into gloves."

Later, when he returned at 2.30 in the morning, having somehow eluded the South Croydon Glove Gangs, I heard him miaowing outside the house, rushed to the front door and opened it – and, I'll never forget, looked out at eye level, confused why there was nobody apparently there. Then I looked down and saw Buster crouching on the doorstep, dirty and scared. Somehow in my mind's eye I was expecting a full-grown Buster, as opposed to this little cat-sized one. Anyway, it took him days to get over it – lying in front of an electric fire while I hand-fed him Kitbits, the living proof that post traumatic stress disorder can be experienced by other species. A week later, while Jeff cleared all his stuff out, and some of mine as it happens, I hugged Buster in the bedroom. And then when he'd gone, Buster lightly hopped onto Jeff's chair and settled down, doing that marvellous cat equivalent of Les Dawson folding his arms and pursing his lips.

Now there was a bit of a hitch today when Linda rang. I've been getting a tad over-confident with the sound effects CD and thought I'd bluff it out whatever happened when I selected a track. I decided, at random, track 15. After all, if it were lovely melodious birdsong, I could say I was up a hill or something. If it was the sound of driving, I could say I'd hired a car. But I got this unfortunately – [*sound of stampeding cattle in thunderstorm with gun shots, over which she has to raise her voice*] which certainly stumped me for a moment, until I said I was at a rather unlikely, um, wild west experience theme park. "Hello? Linda? Yes! Well, it's a wild west experience theme park, isn't that amazing! Ha, ha! You'd never credit it, would you? You'd expect the South of France to be all pots of honey and lavender bags and Cézanne museums, wouldn't you? Ha ha! [*Crack of thunder*] Aagh! Ha ha." I wasn't sure she believed me, so I cut it short again. "Must go! My turn with the lasso!"

At which point the stampeding cattle finished abruptly [*it does*] and in the unexpected silence, Buster walked in and let out the loudest and most unmistakeable miaow you've ever heard. And I said, "Buster! Shoosh!" And then I realised I hadn't ended the call, and I looked at Buster and he looked at me and I looked at the mobile and laughed and laughed and laughed.

Scene Three: next day; cat purring

Day five in bed. Why doesn't everyone do this for a holiday? Stay home and stare at the ceiling? Why don't they have programmes about it on the telly, with Carol Smilie just lazing about between the sheets, no make-up, toast crumbs, six old mugs jostling for space on the bedside table, cat sitting on her head? They could still get all those celebrities on – and the thing is, for once, you could really believe they were having a good time. I mean, what's missing from normal everyday life? Is it sliding down water chutes? Is it cycling across northern Portugal? No, it's this. [*Pause. Sigh*] Staring at the ceiling. [*Sigh*] Eyes closed. Nearby devoted cat purring on the bedspread, teaching by example how to stretch and doze, stretch and doze. [*Deep breathing, as if about to doze off*] Look how relaxed he is. Snoozing in a patch of warm sun. Little tummy rising and falling, rising and falling. Legs elegantly crossed. Utterly unconscious. I'll tell you one thing. Staying at home for such an unprecedented lengthy period I can report that a fifteen-year-old cat is conscious, active and miaowing, in total, for no more than thirty-five minutes in the average day. Now isn't that a lesson to us all?

When Linda rang today, I hesitated at the CD player and then let my phone take a message. What a coward. I knew she'd heard Buster and me. Our secret was out. I'd been thinking it through all morning – dreaming up lies, basically, to tell her there was a last-minute mix-up with the booking, or I'd had a freak burst lavatory emergency and missed the plane. But then, when the phone rang, I couldn't do it. Although the CD would have given me this, [*sound effect of tennis match*] which ironically enough I could have handled. Oh well. The message she left was a slightly emotional, [*choked*] "I give up, Jo. I've tried my best. Don't live each day to the full if you don't want to. Be a cat lady, and I hope it makes you very happy." And that was it. I felt a twinge of guilt, a lurch of compassion and then a wave of relief. Linda has given up on me. Hurrah. Thank you for that miaow, Buster. This has to be the best thing that's happened to me for years.

Just one thing got to me. The thing is, she keeps using this "cat lady" thing as if my flat had forty-seven cats in it and smelled of cat wee and was called Moggy Cottage or something. But I'm not crackers about cats. In fact I can't stand gifts with cats on; brooches, bookmarks, figurines – if it's got a cat on it, I say "Ech" and it goes straight down to Oxfam. I don't love cats, I love Buster. Of course, if she means by cat lady, lady who is also a bit like a cat, whose behaviour is comparable to that of a cat, well, that is certainly what I've been trying to achieve, so I can't deny it. Active, conscious and miaowing for just thirty-five minutes a day? Surely this is a great ideal. Loved and coddled, meals thrown in, endlessly amused by a catnip toy done up as a stick of dynamite? I volunteer for all of that. The only downsides I can see to being a cat are not being able to operate the remote when the snooker is on (which must be awful), and not having hands for a knife and fork at meal times. I really couldn't fancy sticking my head in a bowl and having to manoeuvre the food with my teeth. Looking on the bright side, however, you can lick your own bits. In fact, from my five days of observation, I would estimate that licking your own bits takes up a good twenty minutes of your daily thirty-five.

I'll get up again next week and go back to work. I'll take Linda some flowers and explain I'm ever so grateful but just not worth the effort. Let HER live each day to the full if she wants to, but leave me out of it. I have reached a certain age, you see. They say, "A woman of a certain age" – and everyone nods as if they know what it means, but

I didn't until I reached it, and now I understand that in my case, anyway, it means I've reached the age where I'm certain, sometimes unshakeably certain, about all sorts of things. And if it's been a struggle to reach this stage, at least I've now achieved it. For example, I am certain if I went to the Côte d'Azur on my own I would feel lumpen, pale and hairy in my swimwear, and would suddenly comprehend too late why so many women submit to the horrors of bikini waxing. I am certain I would not float on my back in the swimming pool staring at the blue sky: I'd put on serious rubber goggles that bite too tightly into my face, apply a flesh-coloured noseclip, and plough through the water like a cross-Channel competitor, since that's the only way I know how to swim. Instead of building and maintaining a beautiful golden colour, I am certain I would acquire on my first day red angry burns down the backs of my legs, making the bending of the knee or even the wearing of lightweight clothes an agony for the remainder of my stay. If I drank a fruity cocktail at lunchtime under a hot sun, I am certain I would vomit in the afternoon. And if I met a man who said his name was Ron Weasley, I am certain I would not go out with him. Instead I would exclaim, "But you're a small boy in the *Harry Potter* books. There must be some mistake."

Scene Four: cats yowling sound effect

I just found this on the sound effects CD. It's a good job I didn't light on this when Linda was phoning. Yes Linda, oh yes, er, Ron and I are spending the day at a cat circus, so French don't you think? [*Big yowl*] There's the one on the trapeze now. [*Crescendo of miaows*] Ron, look how the pussycat pyramid tumbles in disarray! [*Hasty*] Hope everyone's OK at the office. Bye.

I'd have had to confess on Monday morning anyway. No tan to show off. No photos to pass round. No romantic attachment driving me crazy – "Will he phone? Should I phone him? Was it just a holiday thing? Do you think it's significant that he said he couldn't remember anything about it?" So you could argue I've done everyone in Bought Ledger a pretty good turn by not leaving the flat. The times I've had to smile and nod over bad flashlit pictures of unknown sunburned half-naked people met on other people's holidays, usually with raised beer bottles in their hands. "So he was the one from Colchester?" I say, attempting to sound remotely interested. "Sorry, of course, Swindon. Yes, I've got it now. So what does that tattoo say?" Hilarious tales are always told of these Swindon people who drank too much, really knocked it back, sank some. Tales in which a late hour, a swimming pool, a crazy dare, and some unexpected broken glass usually feature in a new and exciting combination.

Buster just came in and rubbed his face along my leg, marking me with a scent that luckily I can't detect. People who don't like cats are always quick to point out the realities of feline behaviour. Jeff did it all the time. "You see the way he's rubbing against you – that isn't affection, you know, Jo." "I know." "You see the way he's jumped on your lap, that's only because you're a source of warmth." "I know." "Cats are incredibly selfish and they never really trust you, even if you love them and care for them all their lives." "I know." And then there's the crowning argument from the anti-pet league. "You shouldn't get so attached to an animal, you know Jo, because inevitably he'll die and it will break your heart."

At which I usually say, "Oh my God, that never occurred to me. Buster, why didn't you warn me when we first got together that this dying thing was on the cards?"

[*Yawn*] My last day in bed. If I were still keeping up the pretence for Linda – I had it all worked out – I'd be playing this this evening [*very faint sound effect, "Cabbage White lifting off from the roof of Broadcasting House"*]. She'd be expecting a disco or a jazz band, but I found this earlier on track 21 [*repeat of effect*] and I find it incredibly beautiful. They say that on holiday your senses get heightened, and you get a new view of your life, and it's certainly happened to me this week, lying here day after day with my eyes closed, with just Buster breathing next to me. I could feel the warmth of his little body. Hear him, feel him. I've never had so much space to listen. [*Repeat of effect*] It's like a soul ascending. There are different ways of living each day to the full. That's what I'll tell Linda tomorrow. There are different ways of accepting who you are.

Cast

The Brother.	**Simon Russell Beale**
The Wife	**Janine Duvitski**
The Son	**Robert Glenister**
The Mother	**Siobhan Redmond**
The Father.	**Douglas Hodge**
The Daughter	**Rebecca Front**
The Married Man.	**Stuart Milligan**
The Sister.	**Lindsey Coulson**
The Husband	**Peter Capaldi**
The Other Woman.	**Lesley Manville**
The Pedant	**Stephen Tompkinson**
The Cat Lover	**Dawn French**

Available from BBC Audiobooks

LYNNE TRUSS

Eats, Shoots & Leaves

The Zero Tolerance Approach to Punctuation

Over 3 million copies sold worldwide

Anxious about the apostrophe? Confused by the comma? Or just plain stumped by the semi-colon?

Join Lynne Truss, self-confessed punctuation stickler, in this impassioned and hilarious tour through the rules of punctuation. A runaway bestseller, it is both a brilliantly clear guide for the punctuation challenged and enthralling entertainment for the grammar devotee.

'A punctuation repair kit. Passionate and witty . . . fresh and funny'   *Independent*

'Truss deserves to be piled high with honours'
                                        JOHN HUMPHRYS, *Sunday Times*

LYNNE TRUSS

Talk to the Hand

The Utter Bloody Rudeness of
Everyday Life
(or six good reasons to stay home
and bolt the door)

This is not a book about manners, nor a book about
etiquette. It is a book about rudeness.

Lynne Truss, bestselling author of *Eats, Shoots and Leaves*
and champion of correct punctuation, returns to fight for
the cause of politeness. A joyous rant against the everyday
institutionalised rudeness we've all become accustomed
to, *Talk to the Hand* brilliantly dissects the incivilities of
modern life. Why are other people so crass, selfish and
inconsiderate? Why do we have to put up with so much
swearing? And whatever happened to public-spiritedness?

'A lively and witty broadside against the modern "eff off"
society'   *Sunday Express*

'Trademark Truss ... (very) readable, (very) funny, (very)
engaging'   *Observer*

LYNNE TRUSS

Get Her Off the Pitch!
How Sport Took Over My Life

Get Her Off the Pitch! is the story of one woman's foray into the very masculine and rather baffling world of sport. Lynne Truss spent four years as an unlikely sports writer for *The Times*. It was a job that took her around the world (via the most difficult journeys and least glamorous hotels) and introduced her to some of the greatest living sportsmen (and many argumentative men with clipboards).

It is a hilarious, perceptive and at times moving account of those four strange years. It is perfect for those for whom sport is a matter of life and death, for those who have no idea what all the fuss is about – and for everyone in between.

'Who will want to read this book? Just people like me who are largely indifferent to sport but enjoy literate, amusing, properly punctuated writing about anything'   *Daily Mail*

'She can write comedy for Britain'   *The Times*

LYNNE TRUSS

Making the Cat Laugh

One Woman's Journal of Single Life
on the Margins

A brilliant collection of Lynne Truss's journalism – recording the life of a metropolitan refugee from coupledom.

For seven years Lynne Truss, in columns for *The Listener*, *The Times* and *Woman's Journal*, tried to make her cat laugh. Along the way, 'Margins', 'Single of Life' and 'One Woman's Journal' collected a band of devoted fans, yet the cat remained unimpressed. But, under headings such as 'The Single Woman Considers Going Out but Doesn't Fancy the Hassle' and 'The Single Woman Stays at Home and Goes Quietly Mad', we discover a writer not only obsessed with cats, but prone to overreacting generally – to news stories, shopping, passive smoking, Christmas, coupledom, boyfriends, snails, sheds, Andre Agassi, cooking instructions, requests of 'How's the novel going?' and personal remarks of any kind.

'A small masterpiece of comedy . . . A continual hoot'
The Times

'Trenchant writing, invigorating valour, and a shrewdly observant wit' *Scotland on Sunday*